JENNIE

Jane Claypool Miner

A *SUNFIRE* Book

SCHOLASTIC INC.
New York Toronto London Auckland Sydney

For Davy DuVivier
With Love

ISBN 0-590-42015-1

12 11 10 9 8 7 6 5 4 3 2   9/8 0 1 2 3 4/9

Printed in the U.S.A.   01

First Scholastic printing, June 1989

JENNIE

SUNFIRE

AMANDA by Candice F. Ransom
SUSANNAH by Candice F. Ransom
ELIZABETH by Willo Davis Roberts
DANIELLE by Vivian Schurfranz
JOANNA by Jane Claypool Miner
JESSICA by Mary Francis Shura
CAROLINE by Willo Davis Roberts
KATHLEEN by Candice F. Ransom
MARILEE by Mary Francis Shura
LAURA by Vivian Schurfranz
EMILY by Candice F. Ransom
JACQUELINE by Jeffie Ross Gordon
VICTORIA by Willo Davis Roberts
CASSIE by Vivian Schurfranz
ROXANNE by Jane Claypool Miner
MEGAN by Vivian Schurfranz
SABRINA by Candice F. Ransom
VERONICA by Jane Claypool Miner
NICOLE by Candice F. Ransom
JULIE by Vivian Schurfranz
RACHEL by Vivian Schurfranz
COREY by Jane Claypool Miner
HEATHER by Vivian Schurfranz
GABRIELLE by Mary Francis Shura
MERRIE by Vivian Schurfranz
NORA by Jeffie Ross Gordon
MARGARET by Jane Claypool Miner
JOSIE by Vivian Schurfranz
DIANA by Mary Francis Shura
RENEE by Vivian Schurfranz
JENNIE by Jane Claypool Miner

Chapter One

JENNIE! Jennie Brooks! Wait a minute!"

Jennie turned as she stepped off the train and looked down the tracks to see where the voice was coming from. She saw a tall young man in a gray jacket walking toward her. He was carrying two suitcases and smiling broadly as he drew near.

"Jennie, don't you remember me? It's me, Jim Hurst."

Jennie laughed and admitted, "I didn't recognize you, Jim. You've changed."

"I've been away to college," Jim said proudly. "I guess you've heard."

"Yes, I have." Jennie said, hoping her voice was noncommittal. The truth was that folks in Johnstown made jokes about how often Jim's proud parents mentioned that he had a two-year scholarship to the Pittsburgh Academy of Engineering. People said the Hursts were as proud of their son's accomplishment as if he'd been studying law at Princeton.

"You've changed, too," Jim said. "But I recognized the red curls." Then he smiled so broadly that she had to smile back. He added, "And the dimples."

"I don't have dimples anymore."

"Yes, you do. How are you, Jennie? Say! You're not alone, are you?"

"Yes, I am." She answered somewhat defiantly, because she had an idea Jim might not approve of that. Not many sixteen-year-old girls were allowed to ride trains alone, even for the short trip from Johnstown to South Fork.

"Going to visit your aunts?"

"My aunt Hester is ill," Jennie said. That would explain why she'd been allowed to travel alone. She hated the idea of Jim telling his parents he'd met her. They would be sure to criticize her mother for permitting the journey. That was the trouble with living in a small town. Everyone knew everyone's business. Right now, for instance, she knew Jim was on his way to his new position as assistant engineer at the South Fork Fishing and Hunting Club.

"I'm on my way to my new job," Jim said.

"I guessed," Jennie said shortly. "It was nice seeing you again, Jim." She turned to walk away.

He caught her arm and said, "Slow down a minute, Jennie. You're not mad at me, are you? I know we haven't seen much of each other these last two years, but we're still friends, aren't we?"

"We were never really friends," Jennie said.

"Sure we were," Jim said. "Don't you remember the summer my cousin Betty stayed with us? How we had that tree house?"

"I was ten years old," Jennie reminded him.

"And I was thirteen," Jim said. "Most boys my age wouldn't have bothered with a skinny little red-head with a bad temper. Do you still have a temper, Jennie?"

"I do," Jennie answered flatly. She was not going to let this young man ingratiate himself by dragging up a dead past. So much had happened since then to separate them that it seemed presumptuous for him to claim friendship.

"You sure act like you're mad at me now," Jim said. "That didn't scare me when you were a skinny ten-year-old, but now you're a real beauty whom I'd like to know again."

"I must go, Mr. Hurst. Give my regards to your mother and father," Jennie said coldly.

"Is that what you're mad about, Jennie? Look, I know that a lot of people haven't been very friendly to your mother since your father died, but that has nothing to do with you and me."

"My aunt is waiting for me, Mr. Hurst." Jennie turned from him and started climbing the steep streets of South Fork toward her aunts' white frame house at the top of the first hill.

She didn't look back at Jim Hurst at all. It was true they'd been good friends that year she was ten, and she'd played with his cousin Betty. That summer she'd been young and carefree with a nice home on Main Street just two doors down from the Hurst house. But by Christmas of that year, her whole world was turned upside down. Her father had been killed, and she and her brother and mother had moved to the other side of town, where her mother ran a boardinghouse to keep them alive.

Seeing Jim again brought back all the old feelings of loss and bitterness about the way people treated them after their abrupt slide into near-poverty. The neighbors were kind at first, of course, but once they'd moved from the best to the worst part of town, none of them ever called on her mother again.

Why should she be friendly to Jim Hurst? His parents hadn't been very kind to her mother. Besides, now that he worked for the South Fork Fishing and Hunting Club, he was working for the kind of people whom Jennie blamed for her father's death and her family's misfortune. The members of the South Fork Fishing and Hunting Club were the biggest factory owners of Pennsylvania.

Her father had died working to defend the property of a rich factory owner named Anthony Wright. Two days after the funeral, Mr. Wright had turned the Brooks out of their home without an extra dollar to pay their moving expenses. Jennie had been ten, but she'd clearly understood that the rich factory owners were the enemies of the poor workers. If Jim Hurst couldn't understand that, he was no friend of hers.

Chapter Two

JENNIE knocked loudly and called, "Aunt Nettie! Aunt Nettie!"

Jennie waited anxiously until her aunt opened the door. The little woman was frowning and shaking her head while she kissed her niece and led her into the parlor.

As she was taking Jennie's cloak and settling her into a large, velvet-covered, plush chair, the older woman chattered and scolded her niece. "Child, you shouldn't be traveling alone like this. I've told your mother a thousand times that a sixteen-year-old girl has no business gallivanting around the country by herself and riding public transportation."

Jennie laughed lightly and lifted a hand in protest, hoping she could stop her aunt's chatter, but Aunt

Nettie ignored her and went on, "No young girl of good breeding rides a train alone. I can't think what your mother was doing, letting you come alone."

Jennie had been afraid that Jim Hurst might make that same judgment, but coming from her aunt it seemed silly. She shook her head impatiently and ran her fingers through her dark red curls to comb the tangles out. She could see her reflection in a gilt mirror that hung over her aunt's mantel. Had Jim been telling the truth when he said she was a beauty?

It was hard to see herself objectively. She knew that some people were beginning to call her pretty, but why? Her cheeks were extra pink from the wind but except for that, she looked normal. She saw the same light gray-green eyes and the same heart-shaped face. She had the same cleft in her chin and dimples in her cheeks. Jim had looked for the dimples. She tried smiling at her own reflection, hoping her aunt would think the smile was intended for her.

"I just don't understand how your mother could permit it," her aunt repeated.

Jennie tried to keep her voice from sounding impatient as she said, "Aunt Nettie, everyone rides the train these days, and South Fork is only fourteen miles from Johnstown."

"But you're only sixteen years old," Aunt Nettie complained.

Jennie rose from her chair and kissed her aunt on the cheek. She kept her voice kind as she said, "Things have changed since you were a girl. This is 1889. Besides," she added in her most logical manner, "you sent me that telegram yourself. You're the one who said that I ought to come. How is Aunt Hester?"

Aunt Nettie began wringing her hands as she walked toward the parlor window. She pulled back one corner of the dusty-rose velvet drape and looked into the street below. Then she said, "I'm afraid it is something serious. I want Hester home in bed, where she belongs."

"You mean she's not at home?" Jennie slipped her hand into the pocket of her gray dress and touched the urgent telegram which she'd received hours before.

The telegram said: *Hester very ill. Send Jennie.*

"Mother and I decided Aunt Hester had to be sick in bed," Jennie said. "We knew she'd never let you send for me to take her place while she was still on her own two feet. How did you send the telegram if Aunt Hester was working?"

Nettie smiled at her own cleverness. "I asked Bill to send it before he went off to his daughter's in Pittsburgh."

Nettie was obviously very pleased at the way she'd pulled the wool over her sister's eyes. Aunt Hester and Aunt Nettie had lived together all of their lives in the home in which they'd been born.

The two sisters were nothing at all alike. Nettie was a shy, ladylike, little woman with faded red hair who worried all the time. Hester's hair was a brighter red, and she walked with a determination that few people could match. Though the two sisters were close to the same age, their temperaments were so different that it sometimes seemed as though Nettie were Hester's mother.

On the other hand, there were times when it seemed that Hester was the older. It had been Hester who got herself a position as telegraph operator when their small inheritance began to run out. This act dismayed everyone in the family because the few women in Johnstown who worked were teachers. No one had ever heard of a female telegraph operator.

After six years Nettie was still trying to persuade her sister to give it up, despite the obvious money problems they would have if she succeeded. Nettie had fallen into such a habit of nagging and repeating herself that it was hard to remember to pay attention to her at all.

Jennie loved both her aunts, but Aunt Hester was by far her favorite. It bothered her a little when people said she looked like her aunt Nettie. The little woman fretted so about everything, but Jennie could see it was true that they had the same heart-shaped faces and straight noses. Nettie had been a pretty girl once, but she was a worried, drab little woman now.

When Jennie was an adult she hoped to be like Hester and make her own way in the world. She would like to be married some day, but also wanted to have some independence. She certainly didn't want to be like Nettie.

One of the things that was most annoying about Aunt Nettie was the way that she rattled on about inconsequential things, and now as Jennie tried to piece together the story of Hester's illness, she had to wade through a deluge of descriptive details about what had been going on in South Fork for the past three days.

Nettie began by describing the fact that Hester had a slight cold and that it had traveled from her head to her chest. Then she went into great detail about how she had applied mustard plasters to Hester's chest and forced her sister to soak her feet in liniment. She added, "I made her a nice pot of hot tea and put a little rum in it." Then she frowned and added quickly, "Of course, Hester and I are teetotalers."

"Of course," Jennie said with a straight face. It was a family joke that all Nettie's medicines had rum in them, even though the woman was sure she was dead set against drinking.

Jennie had now been in the parlor for fifteen minutes, and she still didn't know much about Hester's condition. She interrupted her aunt's rambling narrative again and asked, "But where is Aunt Hester now? Is she in bed?"

Her aunt shook her head no and Jennie asked, "Is she really sick? And why couldn't Bill or Ned take her shifts?"

"Ladies never show impatience, my dear. Let me make my point."

Jennie sighed.

"Ladies never make unruly noises, my dear."

Jennie squirmed in her chair.

"Ladies never wiggle about, but sit in a composed

manner. Fold your hands on your lap, my dear, and sit up straight. Remember the Queen of England."

Jennie folded her hands and sat up straight. She didn't want to hear the story of how the Queen of England had had to wear a stick tied to her spine until she was twelve years old so she would have good posture. She really only wanted to hear about her aunt Hester. She decided to use mental telepathy to influence Nettie's mind. Maybe that would work. Jennie closed her eyes and tried to will her aunt to stay on the subject.

"Ladies never sleep in public, my dear. Look wide awake, please."

Jennie thought she would burst with impatience, but she simply smiled and asked, "Shall I go to the telegraph office and send Aunt Hester home to you?"

Nettie didn't seem to hear her offer. She rattled on, "Bill has gone to his daughter's in Pittsburgh. That's a whole day away by train. And Ned is home in bed, sicker than Hester. He's the one who caused this illness by bringing those germs in . . . if you *believe* in germs, and I'm not too certain I do."

"So Aunt Hester is at work. And I'm to relieve her." Jennie stood up as though to leave.

"Yes, she's working, but I don't think she should be," Aunt Nettie said crossly.

Jennie took a step toward the door. She was beginning to wonder how sick her aunt really was. Nettie tended to exaggerate things a lot. It might be that Nettie's false worries were causing Jennie to miss the Memorial Day celebrations in Johnstown for no good reason. As she'd been traveling on the train, everyone at home had been watching the annual parade.

Right now, Jennie's mother and brother were visiting her father's grave, and Jennie wished she were with them. This would be the first time she hadn't been there to show respect for her father's memory since he had died six years before. Well, maybe helping his sisters was showing respect in a different way.

Jennie's heart softened toward her aunt as she remembered her father. If he had lived he would have found some way to take care of his two maiden sisters and his own family. But he was dead, and they were all having to rely on their own frail resources. She hugged her aunt and said, "Don't worry, Aunt Nettie. I'll take care of Aunt Hester."

"No one can take care of Hester," Nettie said. "I've tried to for forty-three years, and she just goes her own headstrong way. How many times have I tried to persuade her to quit this ridiculous position? It's going to rain, and one of these days the South Fork dam is going to burst, and we'll all drown."

Jennie laughed and shook her head. How had the dam come into this conversation? Her aunt Nettie was really getting quite peculiar about her worries. "Even if the dam did burst — and it won't," Jennie said, " — you and Aunt Hester are a long way from the bottom of the gorge. You can't seriously believe that water would climb the hill and get you, can you? Believe me, I just made the climb, and it's a long way for water to run uphill."

"Hester will be sorry she exposed herself to the dreadful tribulations of working outside the home. If dear, dear Papa were still alive, he would be so shocked, so horrified that his daughter was actually taking money from strangers."

"She is not taking money from strangers," Jennie interrupted impatiently, "she is earning good money from the American Telegraph Company. She has a respectable position. She can do something that not many women can do. She can earn good wages. She is a modern woman."

Nettie looked even more alarmed. "That is what I have been trying to tell you. My dear Papa would have turned over in his grave if he had known that she was going to become a modern woman. And now, look at you, you're following in Hester's footsteps."

"My mother also works for a living," Jennie said. She could feel her cheeks getting hot with anger as she went on. "Necessity forces women to be modern." She thought of how hard her mother worked just to keep a roof over their heads. Running a boardinghouse might be a bit more respectable than being a telegraph operator but it certainly wasn't easier.

Nettie ignored her. "I was telling your mother just the other day, 'Bertha,' I said, 'we have got to do something about the way Jennie tags after Hester all of the time.' "

"Yes, I know," Jennie answered dryly. "Mama talked to me about it."

She remembered the lecture in which her mother

had pleaded with her not to play such obvious favorites in the never-ending battle between the two sisters. And Jennie had agreed that she would not always take Hester's side, and she would try to be kind to poor, dear, Aunt Nettie. And now she was quarreling with the woman. She softened her tone and asked once again, "Shall I go to the telegraph office now? Do you want to come with me?"

"I *never* go there," Aunt Nettie said stiffly.

Jennie thought to herself that her aunt might seem sweet and pliable, but she was really as tough as boot leather. "Shall I go alone and send her home to you?"

"Oh, would you, please?" Nettie turned her small, pretty but faded face up to her taller niece's. There was fear in her eyes that made Jennie's heart melt. She took the older woman into her arms and hugged her as though she were a child and said, "Why don't you make yourself a cup of tea and I'll run up to the telegraph office and see what I can do."

Jennie reached for her cloak, but Aunt Nettie caught her hand and said, "I almost forgot. Jim Hurst is here in town. He arrived yesterday."

"Today," Jennie corrected her. "I saw him at the train station."

"He has a fine position at the South Fork Fishing and Hunting Club."

"I heard."

"He's grown into a fine young man."

"Have you seen him?"

"No, but his mother says . . ."

"His mother isn't the best judge," Jennie

snapped. But she added, "He did look fine, though."

"Good manners?"

"Better than mine," Jennie teased.

"Did he ask to call on you?"

"Of course not!"

"He'll do very well now that he's an engineer. Folks say that Robert Matthews has personally taken an interest in him."

"Robert Matthews is just one more villain who made a fortune off the backs of poor workers."

"Jennie, a lady never voices strong opinions."

"Perhaps I'm not a lady."

"Jennie!"

"Just teasing," Jennie said. "I'll go now."

"You shouldn't frown like that," her aunt warned. "Even a pretty face doesn't please when it wears a frown."

"I'll be running along," Jennie said. She had her hand on the doorknob.

Aunt Nettie shook her head sadly and said, "It isn't just the frowns which will hold you back. No matter how pretty a girl is, if she follows these modern ways, she'll never get a husband."

Jennie laughed. "I don't need a husband, I am only sixteen years old."

"Of course you need a husband," Aunt Nettie replied. "All young ladies want a husband, and sixteen is not as young as you might think it is. Before you know it, it's too late."

Then, as though she might have betrayed too much about herself, Aunt Nettie looked across to the other side of the room, went over to a vase filled with wire flowers, and began rearranging them fussily. As she worked on the flowers she rattled on, "A man likes a ladylike woman. A man doesn't like a woman that goes gallivanting around on trains and sends telegrams and talks about being modern all of the time."

Jennie laughed. "That may have been true when you were a girl, Aunt Nettie, but this is the age of progress."

"There is no such thing as progress when it comes to men and women," Aunt Nettie replied snappishly. "Men and women are *always* the same. A man takes care of his wife, and a woman's place is in the home."

Jennie wrapped her cloak tightly around her shoulders and prepared to leave. She said, "Don't worry about Aunt Hester. I'm sure it's only a bad cold."

"How would you know?" Aunt Nettie accused. "You've been wasting time talking when you should be seeing to your poor, sick aunt."

As Jennie stepped out the door, Aunt Nettie said, "I don't think it's cholera, but if it is, it will be because of her own foolishness."

Chapter
Three

THE path from her aunt's house to the telegraph office was steep, and Jennie descended very carefully. Though it hadn't rained yet that day there had been eight inches of rain earlier that week, and all the cobblestones were slippery and muddy. If she broke her leg she'd be of no use to anyone.

As she picked her way down the hill, she wondered how a woman like Nettie Brooks could stay single all her life and be so certain about what men wanted in a wife.

Some of her aunt's views made her want to laugh, but she knew there was a lot of truth in them as well. Men did seem to prefer quiet, ladylike girls, and she knew she was much too outspoken to qualify as a special friend of any of the boys she knew. Even

Jim Hurst had asked about her temper, and she hadn't talked to him for years.

Well it was all right with her if the boys didn't approve of her outspoken ways. She wouldn't play a part for anyone. Perhaps she really would follow in her aunt Hester's footsteps.

Why had Aunt Nettie mentioned Jim Hurst at all? Just because he was a nice-looking, successful young man, did that mean she was supposed to fall all over herself to please him? Still, she hoped Jim didn't think her too rude. She would hate for it to get back to her mother that she lacked manners.

Jennie walked carefully down the hill, passing little houses that clung to the sides of the slopes. There were very few bushes or trees — just the houses perched precariously on the hillside. Their front and backyards seemed like postage stamps stuck on the side of the hill.

As she turned the corner into the telegraph office yard she could see down the gorge to the railroad station, where she'd met Jim. Would he take a buggy up to the South Fork Fishing and Hunting Club? Or was he important enough for the special carriage they kept to meet members who came in on the train?

The telegraph office was at the top of a large wooden platform. She had to climb three flights of wooden stairs up to a large room, where Aunt Hester worked. She shared the job with three other people, and between the four of them they managed to keep the telegraph office open twenty-four hours a day, year round, including Christmas. One of the things Aunt Nettie objected to most about her sister's work was the fact that for two consecutive years, Hester had had to work on Christmas Day.

Jennie knocked on the door of the telegraph office, and when no one answered she walked right in. As she opened the door a little swinging bell rang. She knew it was designed to wake the telegraph operator inside; there were long periods when nothing was happening, and some of the operators were inclined to take naps.

Aunt Hester heard the bell and sat upright, turning the oak swivel chair toward the counter as Jennie approached. She opened her eyes, which looked dull. Jennie was shocked when she saw her aunt's appearance. Her skin was a gray color and she obviously had been very ill for a long time. Jennie stepped behind the counter, placed her hand on her aunt Hester's forehead and said, "You have a high fever. You should be home!"

Aunt Hester shook her head and said, "There is no one to take my place."

"I will," Jennie said briskly.

Aunt Hester shook her head and said, "It's against company rules."

"No one in the company needs to know it. This is Memorial Day. There won't be anyone coming around. I'll work your shift for you," Jennie answered. "You know I'm good enough."

"Of course you are. I taught you myself." Aunt Hester managed a feeble smile.

She had taught Jennie the Morse code the year after Jennie's father died, and for the last six years

Jennie had practiced whenever she got a chance. She was almost as fast as her aunt and a lot faster than some of the other operators.

The idea that messages could travel over wires and come all the way from Pittsburgh or New York was still a new idea to a lot of people, but to Jennie the newfangled invention of the telegraph seemed quite commonplace. Offering to take over the telegraph office was as familiar to Jennie as offering to cook supper or do the laundry.

It took a little while longer to persuade Aunt Hester that she had to go home, but eventually her aunt agreed that having Jennie take over for her was the best possible solution. She wrapped herself tightly in her cloak and struggled down the steps toward home.

Jennie stood on the stairs and waved good-bye to her aunt, urging her to walk slowly, carefully, and to let Aunt Nettie take good care of her once she got home.

It was the first time that Jennie had ever been alone in the telegraph office for more than ten or fifteen minutes, but she was sure she could handle the job. She went to her aunt's desk and sat in the swivel chair, turning it toward the window and looking out on the railroad yard, which lay below her.

From her viewpoint inside the telegraph office she could see the station and the tracks as they followed the banks of the little Conemaugh River toward Johnstown. Ahead and behind her was the South Fork Dam, where Jim Hurst was going to be working that summer.

The river valley was narrow here, and it turned quickly, so she couldn't see very much of the track. She knew the fourteen miles between there and Johnstown like the back of her hand, though. It was the hundreds of miles beyond that set her heart pumping with a thirst for knowledge and adventure. How she would love to see Philadelphia. Or New York!

Travelers who came into the office to send telegrams often said that Johnstown was one of the most beautiful places in the United States. They usually talked about the deep gorge that ran through the valley and the high, steep slopes on either side of the river. Jennie loved her valley and believed them when they said it was beautiful, but that didn't stop her from wanting to see more.

She supposed that was why the wealthy owners of factories had chosen the South Fork Fishing and Hunting Club as a summer playground. Soon these wealthy people would come into South Fork on special custom-built trains and ride up the hill in the Fishing and Hunting Club buggy. They would while away the summer, pretending to be poor people by living in dusty brown cabins. Evenings, they'd gather in the big old lodges and try to pretend they didn't miss the luxury they usually lived with.

Jennie thought it was ridiculous for rich people to pretend to be rustics. She especially disliked the fancy young men and women in their summer white clothes who had nothing better to do with their lives than spend the money that their parents had made.

Jennie gazed backwards over her life, and she

remembered when she had been a pampered child. Her mother had been a housewife, and they had lived in a comfortable home. Her father had been a foreman at the Wright Ironworks, and her younger brother was just a baby. Everything had been comfortable, middle-class, safe, and secure; there had always been meat on the table and carrots in the bin.

Her mother had been a plump young woman with a laughing face, in those days. When Jennie thought back to her early childhood she knew that she had been very fortunate. She wanted that security, safety, and happiness to return.

The last five years of Jennie's life had been a struggle. Her mother had insisted that she stay in school until she finished the eighth grade. Even before she'd dropped out of school, she helped her mother at the boardinghouse.

The boardinghouse was a trap Jennie didn't want to be caught in. If she could have managed to save the money, Jennie might have been able to go to a normal school for one year and become a schoolteacher.

Jennie sighed and turned restlessly in the chair. There was no sense wishing for things that might have been or dwelling on the past. Since there was no money, everyone expected her to work with her mother until she married. But she wanted something more from life.

Sometimes, when she looked forward to her future, she felt very impatient, as though she would like to pack up and run away. The future looked as long and narrow and unforgiving as the gorge that lay below her.

She looked down at the railroad tracks and wished with all her heart that she could find the money to travel. But even if she couldn't travel, Jennie wanted something more than housework. The next best thing to travel would be to sit in a place like this and watch the trains go by. Eventually one of the other telegraph operators would leave and her aunt would be able to wangle her a position in South Fork as a telegraph operator.

Yes. It was better to sit and watch adventure than never to have any taste of it at all.

Chapter
Four

Jennie was startled to hear the bell ring, and she whipped the oak chair around, surprised to see Jim Hurst standing in the doorway. She jumped up out of the chair and walked quickly to the counter, saying in her most dignified and grown-up voice, "Mr. Hurst, how nice to see you."

She hadn't really noticed at the railroad yard, but Jim had grown very tall. She judged he must be over six feet tall. And his shoulders were broad. She'd forgotten how nice-looking he was. He had deep blue eyes, light brown hair, and a wonderful smile.

Now he was smiling broadly, and she smiled back. He seemed genuinely delighted to see her and asked, "Miss Brooks, what a surprise to see you here."

"But I told you. . . ." She realized he was teasing her, and she stopped abruptly and blushed. She was unused to talking with young men.

"How is your aunt?" he asked.

"She's gone home for a while," Jennie answered. She and Hester had agreed it would be better to say she was just filling in for a few minutes, but she didn't think it was necessary to lie to Jim. He might be working for rich people but he was still a Johnstown boy.

"Did you want to send a telegram?" she asked.

"I thought I'd come calling," Jim explained.

Jim was three years older than she was, but it seemed strange to hear him use the words, "come calling." The last time she had seen him, before that day, had been in the school playground. She'd been twelve, and he was in his last year of high school. He'd stood up for her against some bullies.

Jennie blushed again as she remembered how she'd had a crush on him all that summer. But in the fall, he'd gone off to college, and she'd dropped out of school to help her mother with the boardinghouse.

During the last three years she hadn't seen him at all, so it was almost as though he was a stranger. She was amazed at how grown-up he seemed in every way. While she still felt like a girl at sixteen, he had obviously become a man.

He was wearing a dark gray jacket and a necktie, which signified that he had at least managed to get on the bottom rung of the executive position that he had hoped for. She was flustered as she asked, "How did you happen to return to South Fork?"

"I needed to be close to home because my mother isn't well," Jim explained. "When the position came up, I applied. I was very fortunate to obtain it. I have been assigned to the South Fork Fishing and Hunting Club for the whole summer, so I'll be able to visit my mother often."

"That's good," Jennie said. "I'm sorry if I appeared to be in too much of a hurry earlier. It's just that I was worried about my aunt Hester."

Jim's eyes were twinkling as he said, "And I'm sorry I asked you about those dimples. I should have looked for myself."

Jennie blushed again. She wished talking to Jim didn't make her feel so uncomfortable. "What will your work be?" she asked, hoping to change the subject.

"I'm going to be helping Captain Crewel with some renovations that he is doing on the dam," Jim said.

"I'm glad they're repairing it," Jennie said. "People worry a lot about the condition of that dam. You know, there's been talk that it will break someday."

Jim shook his head. "My job will be to repair the docks; but I will be working on the expansion of the club, too."

Jennie stiffened at the idea that Jim's work at the South Fork Fishing and Hunting Club would just make life easier for the members.

Perhaps something in her face betrayed her feelings because Jim said rather sheepishly, "Working to help rich folks ride around in boats may not seem like a good use of my college education to you, but it is a step in the right direction for me."

"Oh, yes, the right direction," Jennie answered. "I expect you'll be president of Matthews Works by the time you are thirty."

Jim smiled, and he said, "Maybe not president, but the future looks bright. Of course, it would be brighter if I had someone to look forward to sharing it with."

Jennie was amazed at Jim's lighthearted flirting. He had changed a great deal in the years since he left Johnstown. There was a glibness, a slickness to him that surprised her, and his sophisticated manner made her feel even more awkward.

Jennie lowered her eyelids, looking at the floor, and her mind raced as she tried to think of a reply that would show that she did not take his words seriously, and also that she was not affected by them. She could come up with nothing at all to say that wouldn't sound foolish. In the end Jennie said nothing.

After a long, painful silence, Jim began asking her polite questions. His first one had to do with her family, enquiring about the health of her mother. Jennie said that her mother's health was fine although she was working very hard.

Jim nodded his head understandingly and said, "Yes, my mother tells me that your brother is still in school and that you are your mother's main help."

"My brother is only ten," Jennie said quickly. She

hated the idea that Mrs. Hurst and her son had been discussing the Brooks family. Then she reminded herself that it was natural for him to hear all the gossip after returning from a long absence.

She added, "Since I've started helping my mother we've been able to open a second boardinghouse next door."

"I am glad you are prospering," Jim said.

"Much better than the first years." That first year, when Jennie was eleven, she had done most of the maid's work after school, and her mother had done all of the gardening and cooking, and they had only just managed to stay alive. But now they had almost one hundred and fifty dollars in the bank and they had the two boardinghouses they were running; things were definitely better.

Jennie was glad that she had on her gingham dress, which, though plain and unsophisticated with the full sleeves and the small pink-and-white checking, was brand-new this season. She was glad that it looked as good as it did, because she did not want Jim to think that she was still wearing hand-me-downs.

Jim said gravely, "I know that it has been very difficult for all of you."

"Yes, it has," Jennie said simply.

"And you really can run a telegraph machine?" Jim asked.

"I learned when I was eleven, right after Father died," Jennie answered. "I can run a telegraph machine as well as anyone in the Johnstown area."

Then it occurred to her that Jim might be in a

position to help her. She asked him, "You wouldn't know of anyone who is in need of a telegraph operator, would you?"

"Are you thinking of giving up the boardinghouse business to go into commercial work, then?" Jim asked.

Immediately Jennie regretted her question. She was afraid that it would somehow get back to Aunt Nettie or her mother, and there would be a big scene over nothing. There weren't any positions available so it was all just a daydream. She shrugged her shoulders and said, "Eventually, it might be a possibility. I'm not certain."

"A pretty girl like you shouldn't have to work at anything," Jim said.

Jennie answered stiffly, "I enjoy working, and what I look like shouldn't have anything to do with that."

"Your brother will soon be old enough to go to work," Jim suggested. "I might be able to help *him* obtain a position."

"Peter is too young," Jennie answered. "We want him to get a good education."

Jim nodded in agreement. His parents had felt the same way, and they had poured all their resources into helping him. "Things will work out, I'm sure."

Jennie would have liked to ask Jim why he felt so sure, but she was afraid he would say something else silly so she dropped the subject. "Look, it's beginning to rain again."

"So it is," Jim answered. "I'll have a wet drive

up to the club. Old Jerry will no doubt bring the buggy."

"It's been raining a lot off and on. I hope we don't have any more flooding this month."

"Chances are we will," Jim answered. Then he asked, "You said people are talking about how the South Fork dam is going to burst?"

Jennie answered, "It's not as silly an idea as you make it seem. After all, the dam's four hundred feet higher than Johnstown, and if it did break, it would really be awful. Then there was Mister Morrell's report. Remember?"

Jim laughed again and said, "Oh yes, Mister Morrell's famous report. Morrell was a tired and bitter old man at the time he wrote that report."

"You're just saying that because you work for the South Fork Fishing and Hunting Club," Jennie answered. "Mister Morrell knew exactly what he was doing when he wrote that report. A *lot* of people around here are afraid."

"A lot of people around here are afraid of everything," Jim answered. "It's because they don't understand progress. We live in the age of progress — every week people are inventing new things, and it's just too hard for people to keep up with what is going on."

"That's *not* a modern dam. It was built over fifty years ago."

"The dam is safe. When Congressman John Reilly bought it in 1875 he paid almost $200,000 for repairs."

Jennie wasn't certain why she bothered to argue

with Jim. He certainly knew a lot more about dams than she did, but his attitude of defending rich people was very annoying. So she continued voicing arguments she didn't really believe. "They say the dam holds too much water."

"It's the largest earthenware dam in the nation," Jim said. "It can hold plenty of water."

"There was no reason to make a dam like that except for the selfish pleasure of rich people," Jennie accused.

Jim laughed aloud and said with twinkling eyes, "Why do people always call pleasure selfish when it's rich people who are having the fun?" He laughed again and shook his head and said, "Johnstown will never change."

"You needn't think you're so high and mighty just because you went off to college, Jim Hurst," Jennie snapped. "And you needn't think that just because you work for those rich folk that they are your friends. They'll turn on you just as fast as anything. As soon as you're not useful to them."

Jim nodded his head in quick agreement, "Yes, you are right about that, but I intend to be useful to them for a good long while. I'm going places, Jennie. I'm really going to get ahead in the world. You wait and see. One of these days I'll be able to offer a girl everything she could ever have dreamed of."

"Well you won't offer it to me," Jennie snapped, "because I'm not interested in dreaming about anything that comes through robbers or rich people."

"I don't know what you are getting so upset

about," Jim said. He looked as though he was getting angry as well, but then he laughed. "Here I talked Old Jerry into waiting an hour so I could come talk to you, and within three minutes we're in a fight over something neither of us can control."

"You may not think you have any control over who you work for, but I certainly do," Jennie retorted. She didn't know why she was feeling so quarrelsome, but she suspected it was because Jim kept flirting with her when he probably didn't mean a word of it.

Jim shook his head. "They say that redheads are quarrelsome, but I'm surprised at just *how* quarrelsome you have turned out to be. I remember you as a sweet little girl with big gray eyes. A kind of shy person. Look at you now. You're a real modern woman, aren't you, Jennie Brooks? Running a telegraph machine and picking fights with the first man who has come courting all day long. At least I suppose I'm the first?"

"Don't try to make fun of me, Jim," Jennie answered. "Why don't you just go on up to the club and talk to some of those fancy girls up there with their parasols and their silk dresses?"

"There aren't any fancy girls with silk dresses that are as pretty as you," Jim answered. "But I have got to go up to South Fork. I'd like to come calling tomorrow night if that's all right. You'll still be visiting your aunts, won't you?"

"Of course not," Jennie answered. She was angry but she couldn't tell if it was at Jim or at herself for getting flustered.

" 'Of course not' means you're not going to be at your aunts? Or does it mean you don't want me to call?" Jim asked.

"I don't want you to call," Jennie answered. "I just don't think we have anything to say to each other. We have nothing in common."

Jim was really laughing now, and he said, "Well, we have some things in common. We're both from Johnstown, and we're both young, and we're stuck in South Fork."

"We have nothing at all in common," Jennie repeated.

"I could make a social visit to your aunt Nettie and aunt Hester, and we could take a walk."

"No, thank you," Jennie answered.

"All right," Jim said agreeably. He bowed slightly from the waist, and, still smiling, he said, "It was good to see you again, Jennie. I just wish you were as sweet as you looked." And with that he walked out the door.

Chapter
Five

A few minutes later, Willie Murphy, who lived next door to her aunts, came to the telegraph office with a pot of hot soup and some cold chicken for Jennie's dinner. He seemed very glad to see Jennie and reported that Aunt Hester was in bed sound asleep.

"Then she's probably all right," Jennie said. She was having a hard time concentrating on anything but the frustrating conversation she'd just had with Jim Hurst. Had he really talked Old Charlie into waiting so he could talk to her? Why had he bothered? And why had she let her temper rule her in that way?

Willie laughed. "Your aunt Nettie expects the worst, but Doctor Campbell came by and said that it's no more than a bad case of the flu. Your aunt Hester should be up and around in three or four days, there is no doubt about that."

Jennie gave a sigh of relief. If she was going to be in South Fork for three or four days she would possibly have a chance to talk to Jim again. She really should apologize for arguing about the South Fork dam. She thought people were silly to worry about it, too. Next time she wouldn't lose her temper. She would show him how grown-up and dignified she really was.

Jennie was always glad to see Willie, and she was glad to have dinner because she had left Johnstown without any thought of breakfast. She begged Willie to stay and tell her all of the gossip while she ate. So Willie leaned on the counter and told her the latest news about his wife and their three children.

Willie, with his red hair, green eyes, and freckles, was the type of man whose face radiated happiness. His ears stuck out, and although he was what he described as a mud-ugly, he was one of Jennie's favorite people.

Jennie found herself telling Willie that Jim had been by, and Willie wanted to know all about him. "He looks grown-up now," Jennie reported, "and he seems very high on himself."

Willie shook his head and said, "Jim was always ambitious — you've just forgotten, Jennie. He was always a boy who was going to go somewhere in the world. More power to him."

Jennie was surprised at Willie's response. "Surely

you think there are more important things in life than ambition?"

"You sound like you think I should be angry at Jim because he's going up in the world," Willie answered. "Why should I be mad at Jim? He is doing what he wants. I'm doing what I want. Willie threw back his head and laughed. "I ride my train back and forth between Philadelphia and Pittsburgh once a day. My wife and my three kids are standing on the side of the track waving to me nearly every time I go through town. I make enough money, and driving a train is all I ever wanted out of life. I'm not jealous of Jim Hurst or anyone. I am a happy man, and plan to stay that way."

As he finished this last part of his speech, a young man Jennie had never seen before walked into the telegraph office. He stood quietly and listened to Willie, then he said, "It's good to hear a happy man. I envy you, sir."

This young man was very tall, well over six feet, slender, with dark black hair and beautiful green eyes. He was one of the handsomest young men that Jennie had ever seen. He was wearing an elegant gray suit, with a pale cream-colored shirt, and a gray-and-cream flowered necktie, and his boots were of soft, polished leather.

Jennie assumed immediately that he was a visitor to South Fork Fishing and Hunting Club. He walked smartly up to the counter and said, "Good afternoon, miss. I would like to send a telegram to my newspaper."

Jennie said, "Certainly, sir, where is the newspaper?"

The young man smiled and said, "Philadelphia, the *Philadelphia Reporter*."

She reached for a blank sheet of paper and said, "You can write your message."

He shook his head and said, "No, no, I will dictate my message as you send it. Pencil and paper are not necessary." Then he smiled and warned her, "It will be a long message."

Jennie was excited at the prospect of doing a long message for a reporter, and she sat down at the telegraph keys rather nervously, adjusted her seat, put her finger on the small, round metal key, and began tapping as he dictated. "From David Winters to the *Philadelphia Reporter*."

He stopped. "What is the name of this town?"

"You are in South Fork," Jennie replied.

"Yes, South Fork, Pennsylvania." He took a deep breath, closed his eyes and began talking in a loud voice, as though he were making a speech. "Robert Matthews' empire has extended from the rim of Pittsburgh all the way into South Fork, Pennsylvania. In this part of the world, where the people vote the way their bosses tell them, they give Matthews the benefit of the doubt in many different ways. One hears nothing but praise for the canny Englishman."

The message went on for several more minutes, but Jennie was so busy trying to send it correctly that she didn't really pay much attention to what the reporter was saying. As far as she could make it out, the newspaper story was about how well the people of Pennsylvania liked Matthews. Jennie wasn't sure she would agree with that, but she knew it wasn't professional to offer an opinion.

When he finished his telegram he turned to Jennie and said, "You're the first girl boomer I have met in my long career as a reporter."

"You're too young for your career to have been very long," Willie said crossly. Willie moved closer to the counter. "And we don't call Miss Jennie a boomer."

Jennie flushed at the phrase *boomer*, which was a slang word for telegraph operators. It was a term that implied that the occupation of telegraph operator was not altogether respectable.

And it was true that most of the first telegraph operators were men who traveled from one boom town to another. Many of them drank quite a bit and the long, quiet hours alone suited them. This slightly shady reputation of some telegraph operators was the major reason that Aunt Nettie was so upset about Aunt Hester's occupation.

Jennie had been raised to behave like a lady, so she knew that the best thing to do was to ignore the young man's personal comments. She folded her papers and said, "That will be two dollars and twenty-five cents, please."

The handsome young man paid the money and then asked, "Is there anywhere in South Fork where I might get a meal and a night's lodging? Our train seems to be delayed, and it is too late for me to make my appointment in Pittsburgh tonight, so

I might as well travel in comfort tomorrow."

"There's no place in South Fork," Willie answered. "You might go to Johnstown."

David Winter had a way of ignoring the things that Willie said and talking directly to Jennie. Jennie could see that his manner was annoying her friend because he considered it insulting to Jennie. The last thing Jennie wanted to do was to have any kind of difficulty with a customer, especially since she was taking Aunt Hester's place without official permission from the telegraph office.

In fact, this young man looked as if he might know important people in other parts of the world. And though Aunt Hester's immediate superior in Johnstown knew that she was a woman, the people in the Philadelphia main office had no idea.

Rather than create a fuss or draw attention in any way, Jennie decided the best thing to do would be to smooth over the whole situation quickly. She said, "In Johnstown there's a very comfortable hotel called Alma Hall. You could continue your journey again in the morning."

David thanked her and asked, "Do you live here in South Fork?"

She answered that she lived in Johnstown, and he asked, "Does it always rain like this?"

"Not always. It just started about an hour ago, but it has been raining off and on. We've had over twenty inches of rain in May. It looks like there will be another storm coming this way tonight. That may be why your train is delayed."

"Isn't Johnstown the site of the famous 'Pumpkin

Flood'? I wonder if I can get a pleasant night's sleep in a place like that?"

"The pumpkins are all cleared out by now," Willie said dryly.

"That was in 1820," Jennie said. "We've had two or three bad ones since then, though the 1820 flood is the one that made us famous."

"Why was it called the Pumpkin Flood?" David asked.

"Because it was an autumn flood — usually they're in the spring when the mountain snows melt — and the flood waters tore the pumpkin crop loose and spread pumpkins all over the valley."

"Maybe my readers would like to read about the pumpkin flood after I finish the series on Robert Matthews," David said.

Jennie wondered why anyone would find a flood that had happened almost seventy years ago interesting, but she decided to stick to the subject at hand and not be lured into another conversation with David. She said, "The hotels are on high ground, so you needn't worry."

"Will you give me directions?" David asked.

As Jennie was directing the young man to the hotel she thought anxiously about her mother's boardinghouses. If this was a bad storm, there might be more flooding in the basements. Though the boardinghouses were set on fairly high ground, the waters did occasionally get into the cellar.

Only last month the basement had flooded, and all her mother's jams and jellies had been ruined.

Willie said, "If Alma Hall is full, be sure and pick

some other hotel on dry ground, because I heard this afternoon that somebody drove their horse into the basement of one of the hotels on low ground, and the horse drowned in the cellar."

David looked quizzically at Jennie, who said, "Willie's not joking. Such events are common in Johnstown. Our floods are just a part of living there." She could tell by the look on David's face that it was hard for him to imagine why anyone would live in such a place.

She started to turn away from the young man, but just then Jim Hurst walked back into the telegraph office. Instead of turning away, Jennie deliberately turned back to the young reporter and smiled and laughed and tried to appear much friendlier than she had been before.

By the time Jim collapsed his umbrella and stepped into the telegraph office, it appeared that she and David were the best of friends. If David was surprised by her change he did not remark on it. She introduced David Winters to Jim Hurst, and the two men shook hands.

Jennie said, "Mr. Winters is writing a newspaper article about Robert Matthews, and Mr. Hurst works for him. Isn't that a coincidence?"

David turned eagerly to Jim. "You work for him? I'm told that he sometimes comes to the South Fork Fishing and Hunting Club with his family. Have you ever seen him?"

Jim nodded his head solemnly and said, "Several times. He's my employer."

"Yes, but I'm told he is more and more remote

from his men, that he is almost impossible to see at the ironworks anymore."

"I don't work at the ironworks," Jim said rather proudly, "I am a special assistant to Colonel Crewell, and as a part of my position I come into contact with Mr. Matthews from time to time."

"Really," David said with a bright inquisitive glance. "Is it true that he gives out dimes to the crowds that follow him wherever he goes? Does he really carry a sack full of dimes with him?"

"Yes, that's true," Jim admitted.

"And in the recent railroad strike, is it true that Matthews was the one who insisted that the Pinkerton guards be used against the men?"

"I'm sure I couldn't say," Jim said stiffly.

"Well, how about the fact that he is buying up all of the small steel mills throughout Pennsylvania and raising the price of steel? Do you think that is something that is going to get him into trouble with the United States government?"

Jim was angry now and looked very stiff and reserved. Jennie knew he was upset at the direction the questions had taken. He looked at Jennie as though accusing her of having brought this reporter onto the scene. It was almost as though he were saying, What have you been telling this man about my employer?

Jennie lowered her eyes guiltily. Of course she hadn't said a word, but she didn't blame him for suspecting her. She had certainly said a lot of angry things earlier herself.

It was Willie who smoothed the situation over by

bringing it back to the weather and offering David a ride into Johnstown on his freight train. "You can ride up front with me," he offered.

David was obviously very pleased with Willie's offer. He bowed to Jennie and said, "This will make a wonderful adventure for my readers."

David and Jim shook hands. When David left with Willie, Jim turned to Jennie and said rather stiffly, "Old Charlie needed to go into Johnstown for supplies, and I said I'd take a horse up to the dam. So I decided to come by again to apologize to you. It was not my intention to make you angry when I was here earlier. I wanted to renew our friendship, and I don't want us to be enemies. We were friends once, Jennie. Can we be friends again?"

"Yes," Jennie said simply and stuck out her hand for Jim to shake. He took her hand in his and said, "I've always liked you a lot, Jennie Brooks."

Jennie withdrew her hand and said in a level voice, "It's true we were friends once, Jim, but I don't think there is anything that you could say to me that would change my mind about Robert Matthews and his crowd of bullies. He is a mean type; a stingy, selfish man."

"Have you heard that he built a hospital over in Braddock, Pennsylvania, and gave it to the town, free and clear?"

"One good deed and a lifetime of making millions that should be shared with others," Jennie said. "He turned out the troops on his own workers, shooting men for no reason except that they were hungry."

"He will build other hospitals, he told me so."

"And he will shoot more workers if he thinks it's necessary, won't he?" Jennie was hot-faced again.

Jim asked, "And you think that because I work for him I am just the same?"

"I don't think that," Jennie answered honestly, "but when I think about what men like that stand for, I hate the fact that you work for him."

The two young people stared at each other quietly. It seemed to Jennie as though a gulf as wide as the Conemaugh River was running between them. Jim's blue eyes were snapping, and they showed his active mind. Jennie blushed as she realized how much she really liked him and how she didn't ever seem able to say anything pleasant to him.

He said slowly, carefully, "Let's not quarrel anymore, Jennie. Let's be friends." Then he took her hand again and pressed it in his.

Jennie felt a small thrill of excitement, and she was surprised by how warm the touch of Jim's hand was on hers. She drew her hand away slowly and agreed, "Friends."

Jim nodded and said, "Well, then, I can rest easy. I wouldn't want to think that there were any bad feelings between us."

"Do you have to go back to the dam tonight?" Jennie asked, "It is getting darker now, and the rain is coming down pretty fast."

They looked out the window of the telegraph office. It had been raining steadily for two hours, and now it was really coming down in dark sheets of water.

Jennie shivered and pulled her shawl closer

around her and said, "This is the gloomiest, coldest, most miserable May that I can remember."

Jim nodded his head in agreement and said, "June will be better. Today is Memorial Day, tomorrow is summertime."

Jennie nodded and tears sprang to her eyes as she said, "I wasn't home to decorate my father's grave today; this is the first time I've missed it."

Jim stepped closer to her, and for a minute she thought he was going to put his arm around her shoulder. Of course she was much too old for such gestures, but his voice was reassuring as he said, "I know you miss your father a lot, Jennie. His death was foolish and wasteful."

"Oh, Jim, it *was* foolish. You must understand why I sound so angry. I've never been able to forgive Mr. Wright for what happened. Yet I know he's no worse than the other factory owners."

Jim said, "Anger burns the one who holds it, Jennie."

"You're probably right. Anthony Wright isn't losing any sleep over my family, and never has. I should just accept it. But I'm not ready to forgive him, just the same."

"I just hope that someday you will be able to forgive me," Jim joked. Then he added, "I was just a boy when your father died, Jennie. It wasn't my fault."

"But you work for a man who has the same kind of policies. It wasn't fair that my father died, and it wasn't fair that Mr. Wright turned us out of the house."

"Life is not always fair, Jennie," Jim said.

Jennie said fiercely, "Don't you want to change things, Jim?"

"I *can't* change most things."

"You're too young to give up before you've even started," Jennie said.

"I haven't given up. Only my way of changing things is different."

"You're *not* changing things. You're just trying to get the most you can for yourself. But what about the other people? What about the workers in the yard? What about the people down there in Johnstown who live down in the poorest parts of town? Right this very minute the water is coming into their yards and up onto their porches. They'll be flooded out by morning because they can't afford to live on higher ground. Don't you feel any responsibility to them?"

Jim looked at her in amazement and said, "Jennie, are you going to hold me responsible for every poor person in town? I didn't make the world."

"No, but you're aiming for a position of power. You will be in a position to remake it." Jennie stared defiantly at him.

Jim picked up his umbrella with an angry gesture, then he seemed to remember the reason he'd come. "We are still friends?"

"Friends," she agreed. She was certain, as Jim walked out of the telegraph office and into the black rain, that neither of them understood what that really meant.

Chapter
Six

THE rain continued its steady, slow, pounding until the wind began to whip the raindrops against the glass, and it was so black outside by five-thirty in the afternoon that Jennie thought her watch might have stopped.

The afternoon was very quiet, so Jennie took down a copy of the latest novel that her aunt Hester was reading. One of the most amusing things about her aunt Hester was that she read romance novels constantly. She kept the most recent ones on a small bookshelf behind her desk. Jennie had never been in the telegraph office alone long enough to actually read one of the books. Of course she'd never asked to borrow one, because she knew her aunt would think she was too young.

So she began to read about the adventures of Lady Silvia, who was married to Baron Hildebrand, and traveled from castle to castle in Germany. The book didn't seem to have much point. The heroine seemed silly and unrealistic to Jennie, and she was amused to find that her practical, down-to-earth aunt seemed to enjoy reading this kind of material.

Turning the pages, Jennie worried about her aunt Hester's health and about the storm. She wished that her mother and her aunts had telephones in their homes. But only wealthy people had telephones.

About seven o'clock that evening there was a rapping on the door. The bell rang as the door opened, and Aunt Nettie stepped into the telegraph office, carrying a basket full of food. Jennie ran to her aunt and said, "Oh, Aunt Nettie, you shouldn't have come out in this weather! You'll catch your death of cold."

Aunt Nettie began to wring her hands and said, "Don't say death, that is a terrible thing for you to say. Your aunt Hester is not going to die. The doctor was there this afternoon and he said she was going to get well very soon."

"It was just an expression, Aunt Nettie, I didn't mean anyone was really going to. . . ."

Aunt Nettie interrupted her, talking very fast about her fears. She rushed through the news. "Mrs. Bradstreet came to call this afternoon, and she told me that Johnstown is under water. The main streets are already flooded, and the water is on the first floor of many of the homes. I just worry about your poor dear mother."

Jennie drew in her breath to control the sharp stab of fear she felt. Then she regained her senses and said, "Even if the whole town floods my mother and brother will be safe. They've lived in Johnstown all their lives, and they know what to do."

"Your mother is used to having a man make her decisions," her aunt said. "She may need advice."

"My mother will watch for signs of flooding, and if it looks as though the water is going to rise high enough to endanger our boardinghouse, she'll simply move all the furniture up to the second and third floors. She'll manage."

"Perhaps you should go home and see about them," Aunt Nettie said.

"I can't abandon my post," Jennie said. "How is Aunt Hester?"

"Not well. She's certainly not well enough to come back. But your family should come first."

"A telegraph operator has a sacred trust to stay at the post. You know that. If I were to leave, Aunt Hester would very likely lose her position. Then what would you do?"

"Do you think you could teach me to run the telegraph machines?" Aunt Nettie asked timidly.

Jennie was deeply touched by her aunt's offer. It was so out of character for Aunt Nettie to offer to tackle something as complicated as a telegraph machine that Jennie wanted to laugh at the idea. She bit her lip and answered gravely, "No dear, by the time I teach you how to be a boomer the rivers will have gone dry."

"Don't use that dreadful word," Aunt Nettie shook her head fiercely. "No man will every want to marry you when you talk in such a manner. I just don't understand how your mother could have raised such an uncivilized child."

Jennie laughed. "I'll make you a bargain. I'll never say that word again if you show me what's in that basket you brought. I ate everything you sent with Willie, and I'm starved."

Aunt Nettie shook her head and said, "It's not much, I'm afraid. We've eaten the last of the ham, so it's only a bacon sandwich. But there is some of my goat's cheese and some fresh baked bread. And there's two pieces of pie. Apple."

"Sounds marvelous."

Aunt Nettie frowned. "I hate to leave you here all alone tonight. This is a dreadful storm. I just don't know what your mother was thinking of, letting you come here."

"My mother was thinking of you and Aunt Hester," Jennie snapped.

Tears welled up in Aunt Nettie's eyes, and Jennie immediately said, "I'm sorry. I wish I didn't have such a sharp tongue. Really, I do." She was thinking of the terrible way she'd argued with Jim Hurst, as well as her rudeness to Aunt Nettie, so her apology was sincere.

Hoping to change the subject, Jennie lifted the lid of the basket and pulled out the bacon sandwich. She bit into it and said, "Delicious." The bacon was cut thick and chewy.

"Don't talk with your mouth full," Aunt Nettie

corrected automatically, then she shivered and drew her wet shawl closer around her.

Jennie jumped up, saying, "Oh, Aunty, let me make you a cup of tea."

"No, I must get back, Hester will be calling for me. She is sleeping now, but she could wake up any minute."

"I'll be much safer here in the telegraph office than you will be traipsing through the storm on an evening like this," Jennie said.

Aunt Nettie quickly agreed, "Yes, the rain has made the pathways very slippery, but I know my way up and down this path. I've been carrying Hester her meals for four years now, so I'm sure that I'll make it all the way home."

"I thought you never set foot in the place," Jennie teased.

"That's a manner of speaking," Nettie managed a smile and trailed her fingers along the counter where she was standing. "I suppose if I did persuade Hester to leave this position, she'd be very bored at home."

"You be careful walking home," Jennie said.

"I'll be fine."

Jennie assured herself that her aunt was correct. She stood and watched in the doorway as the small woman climbed down the steep stairs. Once she got onto the path that would carry her back up the hill to her home she disappeared into darkness. Jennie shivered from the wet, cold night. The storm was very fierce now.

When she came back into the telegraph office, she

went to the small jet flame and put on the kettle to make herself a pot of tea. Then she settled down in the swivel chair with an afghan tucked around her knees and began reading as she drank her tea.

It wasn't long before she began dozing off. Officially she wasn't supposed to sleep while she was on duty, but most telegraph operators napped during the small hours of the morning.

This night there was very little happening, and Jennie was able to sleep most of the time. There were a few telegraph messages to be relayed from one station to the other. There were three phone calls from worried residents who asked for news about the weather, but mostly it was very quiet during the night. The only real noise was from the rain beating on the windows and the tin roof that sheltered the porch. The sound from the tin roof grew so loud that Jennie almost missed a telephone call at two o'clock in the morning.

A man's voice sounded very frightened as he said, "Thank heavens someone is there."

"Yes, I'm here." Jennie wondered how long the phone had rung before she heard it. The water was beating so loudly now and the wind was whipping so fast that she could hardly hear anything at all.

"This is Harvey, from Johnstown," the voice said. "We heard a rumor that the South Fork dam broke. Just checking."

"What did you hear?"

"One of the Italian workmen who's been up there at South Fork for weeks came home and took his family to higher ground. Folks said he said the dam was breaking."

Jennie could hear the fear in the man's voice, and she also thought she heard a slight slurring of his words. Maybe Harvey had been drinking a bit too much. She kept her voice calm as she said, "I haven't heard anything about any trouble at all. Just don't worry about it."

He sounded relieved. "Any other news?"

"Nothing," Jennie assured him. "I've had no visitors and few phone calls. Everything is calm here."

They talked a while more, and then he brought the subject around to the dam again. "You think that dam might break?"

Jennie laughed and said, "What do I think? I'll tell you what I think. Ever since I was six years old I've been hearing about how the dam is going to break. The people of Johnstown talk about it whenever it rains, and it rains a lot. But the dam never breaks, and there's no reason to think it will break this time."

They chatted for a few minutes, and he seemed calmer. Jennie hoped he believed he'd been talking to Hester the whole time, and she thought there was a pretty good chance that his drinking had clouded his hearing enough that he did.

When Jennie hung up, she sat back in the chair, wrapped her shawl tighter around her, and thought about Jim Hurst, who was up at the dam right now. Somehow the idea that Jim was there made her feel much safer than she would have felt ordinarily.

Chapter
Seven

IT was pitch black by the time Jim Hurst rode his horse into the South Fork Fishing and Hunting Club territory. He went directly to the lodge and asked for Captain Crewell. The maid who was mopping up water from leaks in the roof told him, "He's out at the clubhouse."

Jim knew immediately there must be trouble if Captain Crewell was at the clubhouse in weather like this. Instead of going to his room and changing clothes, he turned, got back on his horse, and rode around the edge of the lake to the clubhouse, which was right at the dam site.

The lake was three miles long and a mile wide in places, and Jim didn't know it well enough to recognize obstacles in the dark, so he picked his way carefully along the path surrounding the lake. Very soon, he discovered that most of the path was too muddy to hold his horse with him as a rider.

He slipped off the horse and led it the last mile. He didn't get lost because there were torches burning at the dam, which led him directly to a group of workmen who were digging sewer lines beside the dam rim.

It surprised Jim that the workmen were still digging at this hour of the evening. Most employers would have called a halt to the work in heavy rain after dark. As a rule Captain Crewell was a fairly decent sort of boss.

He wondered what Jennie would say if she knew his job for the summer wasn't just fixing up the docks and paths for the tourists, but to provide indoor plumbing for them as well. She would probably really detest him, he decided. Well he was never going to tell her.

"Captain Crewell — where is he?" Jim asked a workman.

The man pointed to the clubhouse, and Jim entered the three-story building without knocking. By now the rain was coming down so hard that no one would hear him anyway. Captain Crewell was sitting at a table, huddled in a wool blanket and drinking tea. He seemed very pleased to see Jim.

"You've been to the lake before?"

"Yes, sir. Twice."

The last time Jim Hurst had seen the South Fork Fishing and Hunting Club had been in the summertime when he had come up to the lodge with a message for Captain Crewell. His boss obviously didn't remember, but he'd asked him to spend the night in one of the small wooden cottages that dotted the perimeter of the lake.

That summer evening the lake seemed like a happy, carefree place. There had been pretty young women in soft, white muslin dresses with summery, flowered parasols. One young man with his shirtsleeves rolled up over his elbows had a mandolin, and he sang, while other young men rowed across the silvery top of the lake. Jim remembered the envy that he had felt that afternoon as he saw those young people gliding across the surface of the lake without a care in the world.

The other time he'd been there was as a boy of nine. That night he'd been fishing on the lake with two other Johnstown boys. Poaching was against the law, and Jim had known better, but he'd learned his lesson that day. The caretaker saw them and chased them with a gun. Jim smiled as he remembered how fast he and his friends had scampered down the slopes to South Fork on that day.

"The lake was very quiet the other times I've been here," Jim said. "It looks like it's raising quite a storm tonight." From where he sat he could see out the window. The wind was whipping the surface of the lake into little waves that whirled and danced in the light of the workmen's flares.

"I'm glad to see you," Captain Crewell said. He did indeed seem very glad to see him. "You couldn't have come at a better time, Jim Boy."

Jim thought the Captain's voice sounded different. If he didn't know the man well, he'd think he was frightened or that he had been drinking.

The Captain cleared his throat, and his voice sounded normal as he said, "I want you to take that group of workmen over to the south side. "We've got a little repair job to do on the south side of the dam."

"What's wrong?" Jim asked quickly. Was the real reason Captain Crewell had the men working so late that he was afraid the dam might need repair?

"Nothing's wrong," the Captain said crossly. "Just take ten men. Take Mario. He's the one that reported the leak. See what you can do, Jim Boy."

Jim rose quickly and said, "I'll report back as quickly as I can."

"Yes, do that," Captain Crewell said. Again, his voice sounded peculiar. He's afraid, Jim thought. Somehow, the idea that his boss was frightened amazed him.

He went back into the night and called out to the workmen, "Which of you is Mario?"

The men talked among themselves and then one stepped out from the crowd and said, "I am Mario."

"I'm to take you and nine other men to the south rim. Captain Crewell says you've found a leak."

"Many leaks," Mario corrected him.

"Well, let's go. You pick the men."

Mario called out nine other names, and the group of workmen formed around Jim. He turned and started to lead them across the dam top itself. The men began to talk among themselves and Mario said, "The men won't walk across the dam."

"But it's wide enough for two wagons to travel at once," Jim protested. "There's no danger of anyone falling in."

"We won't walk that way," Mario insisted. "What if the dam breaks?"

"The dam isn't going to break," Jim argued. He used all of his persuasive powers, and the men still refused to budge. Finally he gave up and went back into the clubhouse, where he found Captain Crewell sitting in exactly the same position as before. "The men want to take the long way around the lake. But it's already so late and so dark, I'm reluctant to do that."

"That's ridiculous," Captain Crewell said. "Tell them if they don't walk the dam rim they're fired."

Jim said, "Perhaps you should reconsider, sir. In the mood they're in at the moment, I think they'd just as soon go home anyway. I was wondering if I could offer a bonus?"

"Of course not! Just force them to go over the rim and get it done with."

Jim could feel himself getting angry at the obstinate way Captain Crewell was behaving. He thought of Jennie and wondered how she would want him to handle this situation. Just thinking about her gave him the courage to stand up to his boss. He said, "I want to advise you strongly to offer a bonus. Or perhaps I could just go around the long way and be done with it."

Captain Crewell stood up, dropping the blanket to the floor. He was glowering as he moved to the door but all he said was, "I'll handle this." He slammed the door before Jim could follow him.

Jim decided it would be best to wait for the captain inside. He was almost certain that Mario and the others would refuse, and he thought it best if the captain worked it out without a witness.

Sure enough, ten minutes later Captain Crewell came back in and said, "Might as well wait till morning. Not much to be done tonight anyway."

"Very well, sir." Jim decided the best thing was to say nothing more about the workmen.

Soon after that, Colonel E.J. Unger, who was president of the South Fork Fishing and Hunting Club; W.Y. Boyer, the superintendent of the grounds; and a young engineer named John G. Parke came into the clubhouse.

Introductions were made, and the five men talked about several subjects, including fishing and the forthcoming elections. Jim was astounded that no one seemed to want to talk about the dam or the weather.

Jim brought up the subject of the dam twice, but both times he sensed the others simply didn't want to talk about it. He decided that the smart thing to do was to say nothing. Still, he couldn't resist asking, "What is the water level on the dam now?"

Colonel Unger scowled at him, and Captain Crewell frowned, but John Parke answered quickly, "The water is rising pretty fast. I'd say the feeder streams are pouring about 3,000,000 gallons an hour into the lake now. If it keeps raining. . . ."

"The rain will stop!" Colonel Unger said.

His voice made Jim want to laugh because it sounded as though he was commanding the heavens to cease and desist. But the whims of nature were beyond a colonel's command, and everyone in the room knew it.

"All the same, if it doesn't stop by morning, we may have to open the gratings to let some of the water out," John Parke said.

"Maybe we should open the gratings tonight," Jim said. "I'll be happy to help."

John Parke shot him a warning glance.

Colonel Unger scowled and said in a scornful voice, "I see we have another youngster who's willing to destroy a season of fishing for the club members. Young man, you'd better watch out or you'll be out of work."

"But if opening the gratings will relieve the pressure — " Jim blurted out. John Parke gave him a warning kick under the table. So did Captain Crewell. Jim jumped under the double assault and shut up for the moment.

The men shared a dinner of tinned salmon and cold biscuits without another word about the storm or the dam. Jim and John Parke talked about their respective engineering educations, and the three older men talked mostly about how times had changed since they were boys.

About ten-thirty, Captain Crewell said to Jim, "Might as well bunk here for the night, Jim. Your gear's at the lodge, I suppose?"

"Yes."

"I have an extra blanket," John Parke volunteered.

Jim thanked him gratefully. He didn't relish a walk back to the lodge in this storm. It was as bad a night as he could remember.

The others went directly to bed but Jim sat in the dark, thinking about Jennie. It had been a wonderful coincidence seeing her that day, though he'd had it in his mind for quite a while to see her again. She was just the kind of girl he'd hoped she'd be: pretty, sensitive, and intelligent.

Jim wasn't too worried about the harsh things Jennie had said to him. She had a quick tongue, but that went with her quick intelligence. And most of what she'd said had truth in it.

Thinking about Jennie set him to worrying about the workmen who were outside in tents. If he were boss, he told himself, he would invite them inside on a night like this. No man should be forced to endure this kind of weather.

The storm grew worse, and Jim decided to let the workmen into the house. He could clear them out before the others woke in the morning, and no one would be the wiser. And if he were found out and fired for doing it, well, Jennie would be proud of him.

He wrapped himself in his jacket and opened his umbrella, stepping out onto the porch. The wind was whipping the night with a fury he couldn't remember ever seeing before. It was difficult to make his way to the tent where the workmen were billeted.

When he got to the tent, he was surprised to find only five men there. "Where are the others?" he asked.

The men who had remained shook their heads to indicate they didn't speak English. Jim asked, "Mario?"

One of the workmen pointed down the hill and Jim's heart sank. Mario and the others must have gone home. He motioned to the few remaining workmen to come inside the house, and they followed him gratefully.

Once the five workmen were curled up on the floor of the clubhouse, Jim felt he could and should sleep. He went to his room and lay down on the bed with John Parke's blanket wrapped around him.

He woke at five-thirty in the morning to the sounds of the rain outside and of shouting in the clubhouse. Jim ran down the stairs, expecting to hear the worst, but it was only Colonel Unger yelling at the men to get out of the house.

"I invited them in, sir." Jim said.

"You had no authority," Colonel Unger said. He turned angrily to Jim and said, "What's your name? I'll see that Mr. Matthews hears of this."

"Jim Hurst," he answered. He thought of various things he could say to defend himself, but he wasn't sure that any of them would work. Before he was able to decide which argument to use, John Parke came into the clubhouse.

Parke's face looked grim as he said, "I've made the rounds of the lake, and the water's up two more feet. It's only a matter of time before the dam breaks if we don't open those gratings."

Colonel Unger's face went ashen, and he asked, "Is there no other way?"

"None," Parke replied.

Colonel Unger turned to Jim and said, "You're an engineer. Do something."

Jim looked quizzically at Parke, who said, "The water level's almost to the top. The dam has already got enough leaks to weaken the structure. We've got to find some way to relieve the pressure or it will collapse."

Jim turned to Colonel Unger and said, "I haven't seen the situation firsthand, sir, but I'm sure Mr. Parke is correct. If the gratings are loosened, then a certain amount of water can run through their openings, and that will relieve some of the pressure."

Colonel Unger looked as though he had just heard about the death of his best friend, but he shook his head in agreement and said, "Then go ahead."

John Parke nodded his head and said, "Good. I'll take the workmen and loosen the gratings."

"There are only five workmen left," Jim said.

Parke looked distressed at that news but all he said was, "Come with me, Hurst?"

Once they were outside, John Parke turned a grim face toward Jim and said, "I've already tried to loosen several of the gratings, and I couldn't. Actually, I think it's too late to do anything. Someone should warn the towns below."

"Then you expect the worst?" Jim asked.

"Here are the facts," John Parke answered tersely. "The dam was built of earthenware over fifty years ago, and it has a definite depression in the center. The water is rising at the rate of a foot an hour. What do you think?"

"I think we should get the gratings loose if we possibly can. Why didn't you do it yesterday?"

Parke looked at him steadily, as though deciding how much of the truth he should tell. He said, "I wanted to. Colonel Unger was against it because we'd be letting out all the fish. The members wouldn't like that."

"But he's president of the club. Surely he wasn't afraid to make a decision."

"Yes, I think he was," John Parke said. "And I was afraid to push him any harder. Maybe I should have gone to the others, but I didn't know Captain Crewell very well, and Mr. Boyer's job is to take care of the fish so I didn't think he'd be much help."

"What do we do first?" Jim asked.

"First thing is to warn the people below," Parke said. "Can we send a message with a workman who speaks English?"

Jim shook his head. "I can get to the South Fork telegraph office and back in an hour. I'll just go tell Captain Crewell where I'm going and head out. I'll be back by seven-thirty to help you with the gratings. That's the best plan, I guess."

"Yes. That's best." John Parke agreed. "I just hope it works."

Chapter
Eight

CAPTAIN Crewell didn't think warning the town was necessary, and he told Jim so in no uncertain words. "You youngsters are all alike. Always worrying about nothing. In my day we built plenty of earthenware dams."

"It's not just the earthenware, sir. It's the depression in the middle. All dams should be built so that they're higher in the middle and lower on the edges. That prevents the water from putting too much strain on the dam."

"Foolishness," Captain Crewell sputtered. "Besides, the dam is not our job. We're here to work on the sewers. So set those workmen to work digging those trenches."

"Most of the workmen are gone," Jim answered.

"What? Afraid of a little rain?"

"They are afraid the dam will break." Jim wondered how much longer he should stand there arguing with Captain Crewell. The man seemed determined to deny reality.

"Don't look so worried, Jim Boy," Captain Crewell said. "Do you seriously think that responsible men like Robert Matthews, Andrew Mellon, Charles Schwab, and Henry Clay Frick would buy a club with a faulty dam?"

"They might not know anything about engineering, sir. But I do, and it is my duty to warn the citizens of Johnstown."

"Now don't start that grumbling. I've heard more grumbling from these dastardly workmen about that dam. But they are uneducated immigrants, and they know nothing. I expect better from you."

Perhaps it was the quarrel that he had had with Jennie the previous afternoon that gave Jim the courage to speak up. He said quickly, "I grew up in Johnstown. I know a little of the history here. Mr. Morrell, who owned the Cambria Iron Company, sent some engineers to this site nine years ago. They reported that the dam was weak."

"Daniel J. Morrell joined the club right after that and was a member until his death. He can't have been *too* worried," Captain Crewell replied.

"I know that there has been concern in Johnstown for a long time about the strength of the dam. The people deserve a warning."

"If these fools are so worried, why do they build homes in the bottom of a gorge?" Captain Crewell looked at him over his glasses and said, "Young man, you have a fine career ahead of you. I would suggest that you watch yourself very carefully."

"I will, sir," Jim said, and he turned and walked out of the clubhouse. He hoped that Captain Crewell might think he'd gone back to tell the workmen to dig the sewers, but he was surprised to find he didn't care as much as he might have expected.

Once outside, he stretched his canvas tarpaulin over his head and turned back toward the lodge and the road to South Fork. He made his way down the side of the hill very quickly. He scrambled and slipped in the muddy, slimy soil. His progress was a bit too fast because the road down was so slippery. He knew the way back would be much worse.

Jennie was asleep in the oak swivel chair when he opened the door of the telegraph office. She didn't waken to the bell, and he drew close enough to look at her face. With her eyes closed she looked like an angel. Her heart-shaped face seemed perfect to him, and he was happy just gazing down on her.

Jennie opened her eyes suddenly and sat up in her chair, startled. "Jim!" she cried.

"You shouldn't be here alone all night. It's not safe," he said. Why hadn't he found the words to tell her how pretty she looked, or how glad he was to see her, instead of scolding her?

"I'm safe enough," Jennie answered shortly. "What's the matter?"

"We've got to send word to Johnstown. It looks like the dam may break."

"Oh, no!"

"Maybe it *won't* break, but we've got to warn people."

Jennie felt a sharp, strong sense of fear run through her body as she looked at Jim's fierce expression. His eyes were wide with excitement, and he was wet from head to toe. The light flickered between them as she asked, "Jim, is it really that bad?"

Jim nodded his head and said, "It probably doesn't amount to anything, but John Parke is an engineer who has been there for a while, and he thinks it may break. But we're trying to remove the gratings to release some of the pressure. And if the rain stops that will help, but we'd better send the telegram."

Together they composed a telegram: THE SOUTH FORK DAM WEAKENED AND COULD COLLAPSE AT ANY MOMENT. They sent it to Harvey at the Johnstown telegraph office. Jennie tried to call him as well but the telephones weren't working.

"What now?" Jennie asked.

"Hope for the best," Jim said. "I'm going back to help Parke pull out the gratings, and this whole thing will soon be another Johnstown false alarm."

"You must have a cup of tea first."

Jennie put the kettle on but Jim refused to wait.

As he started to the door, she called out, "Jim, be careful."

He laughed bitterly and said, "If the dam goes, I'm in the safest place."

She nodded her head. "I am, too. But I'd better

call the trains down below. They've been holding them back because of the flooding."

"Jennie, if the dam breaks you'll hear something. Run to higher ground."

"Jim, I'm almost a hundred feet above the train tracks. It wouldn't climb that high at worst."

"I suppose not, but I want you to promise me you'll go to your aunts' house."

"I'm supposed to stay at my post," Jennie said doubtfully. She wanted to be safe. On the other hand, she knew her duty.

"Promise me," Jim demanded.

His deep blue eyes bore into hers, but she said, "I'll have to do what I think is best at the time."

Jim sighed and turned away. When he opened the door, Jennie was startled at the fierce pressure of the storm. The wind blew her against her desk, and she felt weak with fear as she thought about Jim climbing up the hill to the Fishing and Hunting Club. It would be a dangerous trip. She said again, "Be careful," but she knew he couldn't hear her.

The first thing Jennie did was call down to the train tracks and tell the dispatcher that the South Fork dam might break. She said, "If you have any passengers down there, you'd better get them up to high ground."

"I can't wake them up," the dispatcher protested. "Not without authority."

"Then call who ever has authority and get it," Jennie demanded.

"But if I run everybody up into the hills, and the

dam doesn't break, I'm going to be in trouble," the dispatcher whined.

"If the dam does break, they'll all be dead," she said.

"All right," he grumbled.

"And you'll warn the other trains?" she asked.

"Yes. I'll notify everyone in the yard," he answered.

When she hung up the telephone she didn't know what else to do, so she went to the door of the telegraph office to get a firsthand view of how bad the storm was. The water slapped into her face, and she had a hard time closing the door again. By the time she got it closed she was shaking, and she realized she was absolutely terrified.

She came back to her oak chair and sat down with her hands tightly gripping its arms. She realized there was nothing more she could do except wait. She forced herself to make tea and sip it slowly. Then she ate the goat's cheese and bread her aunt had given her.

As she waited and wondered, she thought about her family in Johnstown. Would word reach them? She knew there was nothing she could do that she hadn't done. There were no trains to Johnstown so it was silly to even think of returning there. She told herself that their boardinghouses were on very high ground and they wouldn't be hurt by the flood, even if the dam did break. How much water could there be?

She thought about her aunt Hester and her aunt

Nettie, and she was glad that they were also high up the hill. At least her immediate family were all safe. Then she began to think about her friends and neighbors. Of her close friends, the one who was in the most immediate danger was her friend Millie. Though Millie's parents were well off, they had built their house on very low ground, which flooded often. Of course, the house was brick so nothing too bad would happen to it.

One by one, she recalled the people she knew who lived in the bottom section of town, and she went over them in her mind, wishing them the very best of luck. She imagined Mrs. Rosen, who owned the sewing store, and Mr. and Mrs. Hillard, an older couple who lived right in the heart of town. Those people were probably already on high ground because it had rained so much the night before.

Somehow or other Jennie got through the morning with a little worrying and a little prayer. At eight in the morning all her telephones went out. The storm was so black that it seemed more like night than day, and she couldn't see much out her window. She was glad the train dispatcher had taken her warning, and she knew all the people in the railroad yard below her were long ago moved to high ground, but she wished she could see for herself.

She wondered if some of the people on the train had refused to move? People could be stubborn, especially about floods. Every year when the floods came in Johnstown, some folks caused themselves a lot of extra harm by refusing to roll up the carpets in time or refusing to move the furniture to the second floor of their homes.

Jennie began to imagine that the people in the trains below had refused to move. She went to the window and looked through the blackness but she could see nothing. Then she began to imagine that the young reporter, David Winters, was on one of the trains down below and that she ought to go down there and save him.

She was shocked at the foolishness of her ideas. She was duty bound to stay at her post, and she'd given the people plenty of warning. If they refused to believe the dispatcher, they certainly wouldn't believe a young girl like herself. And as for chasing David Winters down, that was an amazing and senseless notion.

There were very few telegrams sent that morning, but Jennie relayed them as though it were a normal day. Once or twice she tried "talking" over the telegraph wires to other operators, but they didn't really know any more about what was going on than she did.

When noon came and nothing bad had happened, she began to hope it had been another false alarm. It was still so dark outside that it was hard to see much down at the tracks, but all seemed to be quiet. There was very little movement at all.

About one o'clock she heard Willie's freight train whistle and pull into the yard, and she hoped he would come up and visit with her a bit before he went home to his family. But Willie must have chosen to go straight home, something she didn't blame him for in this weather.

Jennie forced herself to go back to Aunt Hester's romance novel after she'd eaten the remaining food from her basket. With any luck the storm would let up, and Aunt Nettie would send her something else with Willie. He had another run at about three o'clock that day, and she expected he would bring her supper.

Chapter
Nine

YOU couldn't loosen any of the gratings?" Jim Hurst stared at John Parke and repeated his question, "Not one?"

"Not one," John said. "Were you able to loosen any?"

"I couldn't budge a one," Jim admitted. "The three workmen and I pulled together. We even tried tying a rope to the grating and pulling it open that way but nothing worked."

"Then it's hopeless," John Parke said. "There is nothing left to do but wait for the inevitable."

Jim's heart raced as he thought of his parents. Was their house high enough out of the flood path so that they'd be safe? Earlier, he'd been sure that everyone he cared about was out of danger, but now he wasn't so sure. The power of this water, once unleashed, was difficult to assess.

"I'm going to Johnstown to warn people," John Parke said. "May I take your horse?"

"Jennie and I sent a telegram," Jim reminded him.

"Yes, but I'll feel better if I go down and knock on doors. I can't tell you how responsible I feel." John Parke looked as though he might begin crying.

Jim watched John Parke ride off on his horse and wondered what he should do next. The idea of going into the clubhouse with the others and waiting for the catastrophe to happen was repellent to him. He stayed where he was, staring at the black water in front of him.

From where Jim was standing, he could see exactly how the disaster was going to happen. There were already several fissures in the dam. As the water pounded against the earthenware structure it would simply open the fissures wider and wider until the earth gave way.

What kind of damage would twenty million tons of water pouring down a four-hundred-foot drop do? Jim shuddered as he tried to imagine the results. He figured that most of the people in the towns would have heard the warnings by now and gone to higher ground. But even if lives were not lost, the damage to property was going to be devastating.

He looked out over the dam and saw that water was already pouring through holes in the sides of the structure. Soon those holes would grow larger, and the whole dam would crumble into nothing. Jim had never felt as helpless or hopeless in his whole life as he did at that moment.

To stand paralyzed and watch a disaster happen seemed impossible. Jim forced himself to turn away from the dam and go into the clubhouse, where Captain Crewell sat in a chair by the window, which looked out over the dam. Jim said, "I've decided to go on down to South Fork, and then home to Johnstown, sir. There's nothing more to be done here."

"The sewers need to be dug, Jim Boy. Get your workmen together and start on the trenching."

Jim stared at the older man in disbelief. Didn't he have any understanding at all of what was happening? "We won't need sewers," Jim said, picking his words carefully. "The dam is going to burst, and the water will run down into the valley below us. There won't be any lake in a few hours."

"Nonsense!" Captain Crewell roared. "I won't accept that!"

Jim decided there was nothing more to say. If Captain Crewell was determined to believe a lie until the last minute, that was his choice. "I'm going to go on down now," Jim said softly. "My folks will need me to help them clean up the mess."

As he slipped and slid down the hill toward South Fork, Jim wondered if he should stop at the telegraph office and have Jennie send another message to Johnstown. He wanted to see her one more time before disaster struck. Though he was certain she was safe enough in the telegraph tower, he wondered if he should try and persuade her to go to her aunts' house, which was even higher on the hill.

Jim stopped at a turning point on the path, looking down toward the railroad yard and then halfway up the hill to the telegraph office. The air was so gray, and the rain was so heavy that it was impossible to see much. Then he turned and looked behind him at the high ground, where the dam held back the lake waters. He couldn't see anything but blackness, but he knew if that dam gave way suddenly, the pent-up water would plunge down the valley.

Suddenly Jim had a vision of how fierce that water would be as it ripped through the land. He shuddered in fear and turned back to look at the railroad tracks. At first he thought he was imagining it, but he began to make out dull gray figures walking around by the tracks. He walked another few hundred feet closer to the railroad tracks and stopped to peer through the grayness again.

His heart began to beat in fear as he realized that he was really seeing people strolling along the tracks. Either Jennie hadn't been able to warn them or they had ignored her warning.

Realizing that the dam could burst at any minute, Jim looked back fearfully at the source of the impending disaster, then plunged down the trail to the railroad tracks. As soon as he thought there was even a possibility that anyone could hear him, he shouted, "Head to the hills! The dam is breaking! Head to the hills!"

Jim ran toward a passenger train that was sitting on the tracks. His heart was racing so fast, he could barely understand what he was seeing when he climbed onto the train and saw that there were people in nearly every seat. He ran through the first car and calling out along the way, "Get out of here! Go to the hills!"

In the second car he found a porter and grabbed him by the arms, shouting, "Get these people out of here. The dam is breaking, and they'll all be drowned."

The porter shook his head and said, "I have no authority. Speak to the conductor."

Jim shook the porter, shouting in his face, "There's no time. Get the people out!"

Jim continued his race through the train, looking back only long enough to ascertain that the people were standing up and gathering their belongings. He jumped off the train and ran to the next one in the yard, shouting warnings to the few people he met on the way.

In the second train, he was met by two railroad employees who took him by the arms and threw him off the train, saying, "You don't have the right to disturb our passengers."

Jim ran on to the next train, where he was able to rouse several people to action. It was hard for Jim to see much in the black rain, but he could make out that his warnings were beginning to have an effect and that people were moving out of the trains into the terrible rainstorm.

Suddenly he heard a sharp loud noise that sounded something like far away thunder, but it lasted too long to be that familiar noise. Jim cocked his head and listened carefully, knowing that what he was hearing was the sound of the South Fork Fishing and Hunting dam breaking.

Without thinking, he glanced at his watch. It was two-forty-five in the afternoon. Then he realized he was wasting time, and he ran to the engine of the train and shouted, "Blow your whistle! The dam has broken."

Jim ran frantically from one train to another and called out his warning. Two of the engineers jumped out of their trains and ran immediately for the hills. One laughed at Jim, and two began to blow their whistles in warning.

Jim ran to the train at the farthest end of the tracks. It was Willie's freight train. He called out, "Willie, blow your whistle, and then head for the hills. The dam has burst."

Willie waved and blew his whistle, then he started moving slowly down the track, shouting to Jim, "I'll try and beat the flood to Johnstown. Give them some warning along the way."

Jim didn't have a chance to tell him it was hopeless, that the flood waters would move too quickly. He closed his eyes and wished his friend well, then he ran back to the train where he'd been thrown out. He had to warn them or they'd all be drowned.

As he ran toward the train, a window opened and David Winters, leaned out, saying, "Hello, there. What's all the excitement?"

"The dam has broken."

"Has it really?" David looked astounded at the news.

"You'll all be drowned! Get them out of there!"

"Right," David said. "What shall we do?"

"Get me on the train," Jim said. "Say I'm your friend. Then we'll get everyone off."

David met him at the platform, and when the porter protested that he wasn't allowed, David said, "He's my friend."

The porter allowed him to enter the train, and then Jim turned to the porter and said. "Hear the whistles? Hear that noise? The dam has broken, and they'll all be drowned if we don't get them out of here. You've got to help us."

Expressions played across the porter's face, ranging from anger to disbelief to fear. Fear won. The porter pushed David aside and jumped off the train. Jim and David didn't bother saying anything to each other, they just started moving up and down the train aisles, telling people to move as quickly as they could.

Some of the passengers moved easily, picking up their hats and coats and heading for the doors. One or two were so panicked that they jumped out the windows. Some passengers refused to believe the young men, because they'd been hearing all morning that there was nothing to worry about.

As Jim and David moved through the train, the warning whistles stopped, and the noise of the approaching water grew louder. By now the sound was continuous and loud. David must have heard the sound, too, because he shouted, "We'd better get out of here ourselves."

Jim called out, "I've got a lady with a bad hip. Can you help me?"

David ran to Jim's side, and the two of them helped an arthritic old lady out the door of the train. As Jim jumped down to lift her out, he looked up toward the river where the dam waters would flow until they flooded the whole gorge. To his horror, he saw that the water was just a bit higher than it had been a half an hour ago. That meant that the water from the dam wasn't flowing as he'd expected.

Suddenly, he understood what was happening and the reason for that loud, continuous roaring sound. The water was tearing up trees and carrying those trees along with it as it crashed down the hill. While that meant the water was moving slower than he expected, it also meant that the flood would come in a giant wall of destruction. The trees would form a natural barricade that would force the water to slow down and would also force it up the sides of the gorge much higher than anyone expected.

His heart felt caught in his mouth as he realized that Jennie wasn't safe at all! The water would come down with a force and a fury none of them had ever seen before. It would splash up the sides of the hills and rip houses and trees from the earth. The whole town of South Fork might be destroyed.

Jim cursed himself for not realizing sooner that this was no ordinary flood, but a monstrous mountain of water and trees and debris which would destroy them all. With a desperate heart, Jim returned to the train to force the last of the passengers to run for freedom.

He said to David, "Get out of here, quick. It's going to be horrible."

"How much time?" David shouted over the noise of the approaching doom.

"Two, three minutes!" Jim shouted back.

"We've got some time," David said.

Jim clapped David on the back and said, "Good man." Then they started pulling the last of the passengers from their seats and forcing them out the doors.

The last few passengers were the worst because they were so frightened. By the time David and Jim had three old men with their umbrellas out the door, they had to step into a river that had escaped its banks and was swirling around the edge of the tracks.

"We'll be soaked," one man protested.

Jim knew they would never have the courage to step out by themselves. They were too paralyzed by fear.

Jim pushed them off the train, and David caught the hands of the first two, leading them through the knee-deep water to the higher ground. The last of the old men fell into the water and was swept under the tracks of the train and out into the center of the flood.

Jim dove under the tracks to try to catch him, but he was too far gone. The black water seemed to grab hold of Jim and suck him into its darkness. He lost his footing and felt the slippery surface of the mud disappear from under his feet. He grabbed hold of the railroad underpinnings and pulled himself upright.

David reached out a hand and pulled him onto the

bank. Then the young reporter said, "We need higher ground."

Jim and David scrambled to higher ground, where the two other old men stood with their arms around each other, crying for their drowned friend. Jim turned helplessly toward the train, wondering if he should have left them there.

At that moment, the train began to move and the water rose to the windows. Jim turned to look in the direction of the onrushing flood and he saw a great wall of black water advancing, almost as though it were a solid mass.

"Run!" he shouted to the people who were close to him. "Run to the highest ground you can find!"

Chapter Ten

Jᴇɴɴɪᴇ had the gas lamp lit because it was still so very gray outside, but it did seem to her as though the velocity of the storm had let up a little bit. During the last few hours she'd had very little news, but everything she'd heard was bad.

The telephones were down, and few people bothered to come through the heavy storm to send messages, but one man came in at about one-thirty to send a message to Johnstown. He told her that he'd been in Johnstown earlier that morning and that the town was very badly flooded.

"Some people are already on the top story of their homes," he reported. "The stubborn ones always wait till the last minute."

"But a lot of people should be moving out of their

houses and onto higher ground," Jennie said. "I sent a message several hours ago that the dam was going to burst. Didn't you hear?"

"Heard something about it," the man admitted, "but I guess most folks don't pay much attention to those rumors."

"It wasn't a rumor," Jennie said.

"If it hasn't happened, it's a rumor," the man said. Then he sent his telegram and left.

After that, Jennie sent another message to every telegraph office in the area, saying once again that the South Fork dam was going to break.

Then she was required to relay a message from Robert Pitcairn to Robert Matthews in Pittsburgh, saying that the dam was going to break, and she breathed a sigh of relief. If Mr. Pitcairn knew the break was imminent then surely the people of Johnstown would be warned and take appropriate precautions.

She sent a message to the telegraph operator in Johnstown asking how things were and he replied, "Water's very high." She began to have more concern for her own family than she had had before.

Jennie knew that it would be foolish to abandon her post at the telegraph office and try to make her way home. Her mother and brother were probably safe. Their brick boardinghouse was halfway up the hill. Jennie could not imagine that flood waters could ever rise high enough to do any serious damage.

The whistles began to blow at exactly two-fifty, and almost immediately Jennie began to hear a sound she had never heard before in her life.

It was the sound of a monster from her worst nightmare. A roaring, slow, moaning, deadly, grinding noise that seemed to come from a long distance off, that grew in volume and got louder and louder until Jennie put her hands over her ears. Still the sound came on, louder, and when she realized she couldn't block it out, she opened her mouth and screamed.

Even as she screamed, she forced herself to look out the window toward the dam. She was stunned by the sight before her eyes. It wasn't a mere rush of water making that noise, but a huge black wave — nearly two hundred feet tall. The wave was a giant black wall of water moving toward her with a slow, terrifying certainty.

Jennie screamed louder than she could ever have believed she could and closed her eyes in rejection of what she was seeing. It wasn't possible that water could stand so tall or move so slowly.

Then she opened her eyes to admit the truth. She was directly in the path of the water. The telegraph office was going to crumble. It was too late to run for higher ground because she would have to run down the stairs and back up the hill. There was no time.

For the first time she understood the tremendous power that was behind nature. She stood and watched her approaching doom with a detached admiration for the power she saw. No one had guessed that the water could come that high. No one had guessed that the water, when it came, would be a solid wall, and not an ordinary flood which rose slowly, overflowing the river banks.

Jennie had a moment to pray, to ask a blessing for her family, and then she felt the telegraph tower begin to rock as the advancing waters swirled around the base of the stilts that held up the platform.

The next thing she knew there was a loud crash and a roar. The platform started shaking, and the floor seemed to slide out from beneath her. Her oak chair rolled across the floor, slamming into the counter and then back into the desk. Jennie knelt down, covering her head to protect herself, and prepared herself for the worst.

She felt the wooden floor roll again, then heard the platform stilts snap, and suddenly the office was falling into empty air. There was a crashing, a sudden recoil, and another crashing into the wall of water.

Water poured through the windows, and Jennie was knocked to one side of the office as the door flew open and one of the side walls crumpled. She saw that her chair and desk were floating past her and that water was filling up the office. Jennie grabbed a tall hat rack and half-swam and half-walked to the window on the side nearest the high ground. She used the hat rack to knock the glass out of the window, and then she propelled herself out of the telegraph office window and into the blackness of the flood.

She grabbed hold of the standing posts on the porch and used them to steady her climb as she scrambled up onto the roof. Once on the roof, she grabbed the metal tube that was the top end of the potbellied stove and held on as tightly as she could.

Clinging to the metal pipe and flattened against the tin roof, she rode the wall of water down the valley. Down, down, down the slopes and around the bends of the river valley. She was aware of very little beyond surviving, but she did know that she was in the midst of a maelstrom and that the water beneath her was thickening with more and more debris as the flood hit houses and trees.

It was as if she were in a dream. She could see a lot of what was happening, but it didn't make any sense to her. Her tin raft skimmed the surface of the water and then began to sink beneath the surface, only to be jammed up against the telegraph office stilts.

Jennie had the presence of mind to crawl off the tin roof and onto the first large wooden plank that she could reach. She had enough sense of survival to know that eventually the tin would sink to the bottom and the wood would float as long as it could.

The water rushed forward, and her board acted like a battering ram, pounding out a path between the water and tree stumps that carried her downstream. She realized that she was much higher than anyone would have dreamed possible. On her left, she saw the tall spire of the South Fork church and she knew that she was above the level of her aunts' house.

Aunt Hester and Aunt Nettie were taken, too! That was the last conscious thought that Jennie had. Beyond that, all she could do was hold on tight, keep her head up as much as she could, and hang onto the rough plank.

She heard a scream and turned her head in time to see Willie's brick house collapse and fall into the black water. It looked for all the world like a child's house made of toy bricks: One flick of a wrist and the whole thing tumbled. One slap of the water and the sturdy house filled with Willie's wife and children tumbled into nothingness.

Jennie couldn't see much, nor could she really piece together what she *could* see, but she knew she was not alone in the black water. All around she could hear screaming, and she saw pieces of houses, pieces of trees, picket fences — everything that made up a village was tumbling in the water. It seemed as though it was a giant jigsaw puzzle with the parts strewn so far apart that they would never fit together again.

Jennie whirled in a circle, and she could feel the undertow pulling her down to her death. Suddenly she spun out of the circle and toward the center of the flood. Things crashed around her. She ducked when she could, took the blows she could not avoid. The water sometimes swallowed her completely and then it threw her up to the surface again. She ceased to fight, but did hold onto the heavy plank.

The noise was so overpowering that Jennie could not think. It seemed as though her breath had stopped, that she existed on the water's power, not her own. The water became the only life.

She heard crashing and screaming as the wall of water assaulted the trees along the banks. She saw people on dry ground, who were running to the hills in front of her. Riding the crest of the flood, she could see a long way forward, but she was too much a part of the scene to understand anything except that at any second her life would be over.

At times she felt as though she were actually a part of the flood, wreaking havoc on the world.

Then she lost her grip on the plank and sank down into the black depths of the flood. She was so tired, so tired of the noise and the fear. She longed for sleep, and she knew that all she had to do was give up, to sink deeper into the blackness, and it would all be over.

She struggled to the surface, catching hold of something, and pulling her head out of the water. She realized she'd caught hold of a rooftop, and with great effort she hoisted herself onto it. She lay face down, exhausted and defeated, and waited for the rooftop to carry her to safety or destruction. It mattered little to her which one it would be.

The impressions she registered were of blackness and power, of fierce, gigantic, horrible sounds. After a while she lifted her head again. Through the rain she saw people scrambling up the side of the hill. She watched in horror as the water filled the valley.

Then the piece of the roof that she was hanging onto crashed up against a railroad car. She hung on tightly as the roof jostled and pushed for a place in the growing mass of debris that rode down the valley with the flood.

She saw a railroad car turned upside down and

people crawling out the windows, only to be sucked into the black waters.

As she held onto her rooftop, she became more and more embroiled in the mass of grinding debris that rode with the terrible water. The wave moved slower and slower, crushing people, houses, and railroad cars as it traveled the valley.

Jennie lifted her head, and she realized that she could see Johnstown up ahead. Houses clustered in the main streets at the bottom of the gorge, and other houses perched on the sides of the hills. She knew that everything up ahead of her would be destroyed.

I'm going home, Jennie thought. I'm going home. She was filled with a sense of great peace and sadness. Soon she would be home, and her home would be destroyed. Soon it would all be over.

Jennie's flimsy piece of rooftop was knocked out from under her when it slammed full-force into a railroad car. She was pulled under the water once again. She thought she heard the screams of the Johnstown people, and then she could hear nothing. Silence cradled her in its arms.

Chapter
Eleven

THE next thing Jennie knew she had hold of a huge wooden log, and she was bobbing along behind the full onslaught of the debris. She was still moving fast, but now the water was more like a lake than a waterfall.

She saw that the wall of water had collected so much debris that it had actually slowed itself down. There was water coming behind her, but it was being stopped by the mountain of debris that was in front of her. She was almost stationary, and she decided to try to make it closer to the bank of the river. She slipped along the edge of the log until she came near the end and discovered that it was really a telephone pole.

Jennie's will to live had returned. She forced herself to keep holding onto the telephone pole. For the first time since the disaster struck, Jennie was fiercely determined to hang onto life.

To live, to refuse to give up, was the most important thing in the world. She clung to the telephone pole as the world collapsed around her. She heard the shrill shriek of a railroad whistle. She thought of Willie and his dead family. She thought of her mother and brother. Were their boarding-houses high enough on the hill to survive? She thought of Jim Hurst and David Winters. Had they survived?

Then a large block of wood crashed against her telephone pole, throwing her off balance, and there was that dreadful blackness again as she sank under the water. Once again she fought the darkness and came bursting to the surface with an energy she never expected she'd have.

Jennie knew she was now hanging onto a large window frame and bobbing along at the side of the deluge, nearer the banks than she had been before. The center of the flood was traveling faster than the edges, and she could see disaster racing by.

She saw a whole house floating down the river. There were people on the roof and others screaming out the windows of the top floor. She saw a dead cow floating down the water and then two more houses full of people raced by. The people had such terrified looks on their faces that Jennie felt even more afraid than she had before.

By now she was even closer to the shore, out of the full force of the storm. She realized that little by little she was being carried toward the edge of the swollen river bank. She might indeed live.

Strength rushed through her, and her mind raced as she tried to think of ways to survive. She looked for something bigger and stronger and more stable to hold onto, but the things that were rushing down the river moved so quickly that it was hard for her to grasp at anything.

Houses, trees, poles, and pieces of wreckage all rushed down until they hit a massive wall of debris. Jennie could see that she would eventually end up as part of the wall unless she found a way to get closer to the shore. The wall was moving more slowly, but it was becoming more dangerous as it thickened and grew in height.

She realized she had only one small chance to survive. If she could get far enough away from the center of the maelstrom, it was possible that she might wash up along one of the banks. She began trying to paddle her window frame toward shore. At the same time, she was looking for an opportunity to catch hold of something steadier.

She managed to steer herself to within five feet of the bank, where she saw some people standing there ready to help. There was a man who called out and reached his arms out to her. She stretched toward him but she was afraid to let go of her window frame. If she let go and the man missed catching her, she would be without any support at all. She was too weak to swim, and the current was much too strong. She would be dragged down again into that terrible darkness.

Jennie let herself be carried away from the people. As long as she held onto the window frame and kept her head up, she had some chance of survival. She rode her window frame slowly down the valley, and when she recognized Alma Hall still standing in one piece, she realized she must be in the center of town.

The realization brought tears to her eyes; her home, and probably her family, too, were destroyed. The wall of destruction that she was riding was turning onto the main street.

In front of her she saw buildings that she had known all her life smashed into heaps of rubble. The destruction moved more and more slowly as the debris dammed itself up. She was aware that the water was rising higher and higher as the debris forced the water backward. What was not already destroyed soon would be.

She could see people on the banks scrambling backward to safety. She could hear shouts and screams from people on the banks and from people who were riding downriver in the wall of debris. She saw several more dead cows floating in the water and the corpses of three women bobbing in the shallower water by the banks.

But she did not recognize anyone, and she did not see anyone actually escape the destruction. It was a horrible sight, a horrible experience, and as she plowed through the city of Johnstown, she didn't want to see any more.

Death would be a pleasant relief after the horror that she was now living. She longed to let go of the window frame and slip into oblivion, into the eternal sleep that she knew was soon to be hers. To give up the pain, the horror, and the certain knowledge that her family was dead, seemed sweet.

Jennie's hold on the window frame loosened, and she leaned back toward the blackness. She felt herself sinking, sinking. As her consciousness faded away the sounds of the horror around her grew fainter. She could barely hear the shrill screams of the people. It seemed good to let go. To let go and sleep forever.

Faintly, she heard someone calling to her, "Girl! Girl! Over here!" A man who was racing by on a wooden bed, caught in the center of the flood, called out again, "Girl! Here, catch!"

The man stood up on the mattress, almost falling with the effort, and threw a baby over the dark flood waters toward Jennie. Jennie reached up and caught the child in her arms instinctively. As she reached for the baby, she had to let go of the window frame, and then she was in the water with nothing to hold onto. She held the baby over her head and began to paddle with her legs to stay afloat.

It was impossible to swim against the current, but there was so much debris in the water that she soon found she was walking on a riverbed of old wood, parts of houses, and tree stumps. Her feet weren't touching solid ground, but they were touching something solid at least part of the time.

She moved toward the shore, holding the child over her head and struggling not to lose her footing. Carefully she put one foot in front of the other, testing to see if there was something substantial beneath her. She could see several people on the edge of the riverbank, who were calling to her to come that way.

She picked her way toward safety, using every last bit of her strength to keep the baby out of the water and to battle the current. While she traveled over the debris, she was also traveling downstream toward the Johnstown Bridge. She worked with all her might but with little conscious recognition of what she was doing.

Everything she was doing seemed as wild and as instinctive as the power of the water itself. It was as though she and the dam waters were somehow connected. Jennie felt a power within herself that she had never known existed. There was a kind of joy at the discovery of the energy which was surging through her body. The most important thing in the world was to save this child, and she was determined to do it.

A chair, floating on the surface of the water, crashed against her, knocking her down. Once again she was struggling with the blackness. She managed to flail around, keeping the child's head above the water, until she regained her footing and resumed her journey toward the shore.

She made slow progress, taking only a few steps before the current would push her backward. She was exhausted. She moved as though in a dream. But step by step she inched closer to the shore. The wall of debris ahead of her was growing higher and

higher and damming up more and more water behind it. Very soon, if she did not make it to shore,
she would be trapped in the horrible mass of furniture and houses that formed the monstrous wall.

The current was too strong, she was battling it
as fiercely as she could. The headway she was making to shore was the best she could do. If the debris
piled up too high or the current carried her too far
downstream, there would be no escape.

All Jennie could do was hold the baby high and
fight her way toward her destination. Soon she was
swept around a bend.

She looked up and saw dry ground in sight, and
there were people calling out to her and several
other victims in the water. She tried to move closer
to the shore. The current seemed to be less strong
than before but the water pushed her fiercely downstream. She hoped to get close enough for one of
the people on dry land to give her a hand before the
current swept her beyond them, but she failed to
make it that far.

Jennie reached a place where there were eight
young men who had formed a human chain out over
the water and were reaching down to flood victims
to catch them as they floated by. As Jennie drifted
near them, the closest young man reached out his
hands and said, "Catch hold."

The current was moving fast, and she knew this
was probably her last chance to make a grab for
safety. But to make that grab she would have to
loose her hold on the baby. Could she hold the baby

with one hand and reach for freedom with the other? She was afraid to take the chance of dropping the baby.

"Catch hold!" the young man yelled. He reached out one hand and held on tight to his companion, who was the next link in the human chain.

Jennie handed him the baby and he quickly turned to pass the baby to his companion. The young men in the chain had to encircle each other to keep from drowning themselves as they passed the baby toward the shore.

Cruelly, the current seemed to be moving swifter than before, and Jennie knew the chances were great that she would not be rescued. When the young man turned back to her and held out his hand, he looked very frightened. He leaned forward as far as he could and called, "Catch hold."

Jennie stretched forward, touching his fingertips. For a moment, they paused, clasping hands. For an instant she dared to hope she was saved. But she quickly discovered that she was trapped in the debris that encircled her. She could not pull loose.

For a moment she held on to the young man's hand and let herself be pulled ahead by the dreadful prison she was trapped in. Then she realized that she would only endanger his life by holding on longer, and she let go.

Jennie thought of the child she'd rescued. She felt a tremendous relief that the baby was safe. She was filled with pleasure at the thought that the child would live because of her.

As the young man reached out one more time to

offer his hand to her, a railroad car came crashing around the bend and up against the side of the river bank, throwing water even higher up against the bank.

The chain of rescuers dodged back to higher ground, and Jennie abandoned all hope of her own rescue. The railroad car moved closer and closer toward her, and Jennie realized it would push her into the wall of debris that was waiting at the Johnstown Bridge.

Her last vision was the horror-stricken look on the face of the young man who had tried to rescue her. She knew by the look in his eyes that it was all over.

Chapter
Twelve

THERE was blackness. Then there was the sound of grinding as the pieces of houses, trees, railroad cars, carts, and corpses of animals and humans slammed into each other as they reached the impasse of the bridge.

When Jennie regained consciousness she was part of a new dam, which had accumulated and been carried along the fourteen-mile river route between South Fork and Johnstown. Once this mountain of debris reached the Johnstown Bridge, it was stopped by the strong bridge spanning the Conemaugh River.

The debris backed up behind the bridge for several hundred feet, and it was packed tightly as new waves of detritus hit the barricade.

Jennie was lodged under a railroad car, against a house, with one arm pinned beneath her. She was up to her chest in objects from the storm but she had her head out, and she could breathe without any difficulty.

Once Jennie regained consciousness, her first thought was sheer amazement that she wasn't dead. She was also amazed that she seemed to be totally out of the water. Gradually, she began to realize where she was and give thanks that she was still alive.

Once she realized she was alive, she also began to feel the pain. Every muscle and limb of her body was screaming with pain. A few agonizing attempts to jerk herself free convinced her to hold very still and wait for help.

She struggled as much as she could bear to, stopping when she thought she might black out again, then resuming when the pain receded. No matter how hard she tried, she was totally immobilized.

She began to hear people screaming in the distance. Then she smelled smoke, and she twisted and raised her head to look out over this giant dam of refuse. She saw that there was a fire in the distance.

At first it looked as if the water was on fire. It was very confusing. How could anything that wet also be burning?

The smell of fire was so frightening! She struggled against the debris that imprisoned her, realizing that she was in danger of burning to death.

At that thought she began to laugh hysterically. To have fought the flood, and survived, only to burn to death in the debris, seemed so ironic it was funny. There was nothing to do except laugh. So she laughed and laughed, tears rolling down her cheeks.

Perhaps for the fifth time, in that terrible journey down the valley, she said good-bye to life. Then, as the laughter faded and the screams of others became louder, she felt one more surge of power, and her laughter turned to anger.

She became so angry at what had happened that she began to twist and flail to free herself. She fought and pulled against the logs. Eventually she got one arm free. She reached that arm up and found another tree trunk to hold on to, and began to pull herself up.

As she pulled, she felt her flesh being ripped away; the pain was horrible, but she continued to pull upward with her one hand. Then she was able to move her shoulder, and her left hand was free. She lifted her left hand over her head and grasped the tree trunk with both hands and began the long, slow pull. She pulled her body higher up out of the pile of debris, but as she pulled, she realized that her right foot was pinned and would not budge.

At the same time she began to smell the flames, and she knew that the fire would be coming toward her within a matter of minutes. She still found it impossible to understand how this soggy mass could be burning, but she didn't doubt that it was.

She heard people close by screaming in agony and she fell into a total panic. She began to scream, too. She knew people were close to her but she couldn't see into the blackness of the late afternoon.

Then in the darkness she felt someone's hands over her hand, and she heard voices. She heard one man speaking to another, "She's stuck. Let's see if we can get her out."

She felt two men taking hold of her hands. They pulled, and she cried out, "My foot! My foot is broken!"

The men each grabbed her under the armpits, and she heard them count, "One, two, three." There was a tug, and suddenly she was free of the debris and in the arms of one of the men. She thought the man who was carrying her was Jim Hurst and she almost felt safe.

Then Jim was setting her down by the bank of the river. He cradled her in his arms and smoothed the hair back from her forehead as he whispered, "Jennie. You're all right. You're going to be all right."

"Jim," she murmured. "How did you find me?"

"I have to go, Jennie. I'm needed," he said. "I'll be back as soon as I can."

He laid her gently down on the ground and she sank into a soft sleep.

Chapter
Thirteen

THE next time Jennie woke all she could understand was that the pain in her foot had traveled all the way up her leg and was nearly unbearable. She called out into the dark, "Jim? Jim?"

"Name's Henry," a rough voice answered her. "See if you can stand on that leg, girly."

"Where's Jim?" she asked.

"No Jim here," the man answered roughly. "If you can stand on the leg, we can use your help. If not, you'll have to fend for yourself until morning."

Jennie shivered and said, "Help me up."

The man helped her to her feet and then tried to support her as she took a step on her foot, but she cried out in such pain that he said, "You're not much good to anyone, Missy. You'll have to wait here till morning."

"I can't," Jennie said. "I have to find my mother. And where's Jim?"

The man moved off without another word, and Jennie found herself alone on the bank of the river. She didn't understand much of what was going on, but she did know that she needed to get help. She crawled toward a light, sliding her wounded foot and leg through the mud.

As she approached the light, she called out, "Can someone help me?"

There were voices, and she could see movement, but no one answered her. She crawled closer and looked at the group that circled the light. There were four women and three men, all wrapped in blankets, and all of them seemed to be in shock. They sat and stared at the burning campfire as though they'd never seen a blaze before.

Jennie called out to the nearest woman, "Can you help me?"

The woman stared at her as though she didn't understand a thing Jennie was saying.

One by one, Jennie asked each of the people in the group for help, and each behaved as though they couldn't hear her. Finally, the first woman said, "Get along, girl. There's no help here. Can't you hear what's happening?"

Jennie didn't understand, but she was so weak and tired, and her foot hurt so much, that she couldn't reply except to say, "I want my mother. I want my mother and Jim. Have you seen Jim Hurst?"

The woman bent over her and glared at her as she asked, "What do I care for your Jim? Can't you hear the screaming? That's my family burning over there. All of my family. Burning!" The woman glared at Jennie and turned away.

Jennie crawled up the bank toward a dark shadow, which she believed was another cluster of people. The pain in her leg was excruciating, and she was exhausted. Half the time she wasn't sure where she was, but the one thought that kept her moving was that she needed to find her mother, or her brother, or Jim, or someone else that she knew.

The ground she traveled over was drier now, and she began to feel safe. Even in her confused state, she knew that the worst of the flood was over. She could hear sounds all around her, but she couldn't really figure out what was going on anywhere at all.

Finally she neared a group of people who were standing in a cluster, talking. She called out, "I need help. Please!"

One of the men ran over to her and lifted her up. He said, "Jennie? Is that you, Jennie Brooks?"

"Yes, it's me," Jennie answered. She wasn't sure who it was that she was talking to.

"You look like you're hurt pretty bad," the man said. "I'll help you to the infirmary."

One of the other men shook his head and said, "Just get her in out of the weather. The infirmary won't take anyone as healthy as she is."

"My foot is hurt," Jennie said weakly.

"Infirmary only takes immediate emergencies, girly. You can rest in the Edwards' house."

The man who had helped her half-carried her into the house and said, "Mrs. Edwards, I brought you another one."

"I can't take any more," the woman said.

"This is Jennie Brooks," the man said. "I reckon you know her folks. Father used to be foreman down at Wright Ironworks."

"She can lie down over there," the woman said crossly. She pointed to a vacant corner of the living room. The man helped Jennie walk to the corner and then eased her down to the floor as gently as he could. He said, "You'll be all right here."

Jennie sank into a deep sleep. Twice she woke and sat up, looking around the house and calling out for her mother. Both times someone said, "Your mother's not here. Nothing to do till morning." Jennie could see that the living room floor was covered with sleeping refugees from the flood.

The third time she woke, she asked, "What time is it?"

"Four o'clock," came the answer.

She sat up and rubbed her eyes, then looked toward the kitchen, where she could see light. Haltingly, she felt for the living room wall for support and, steadying herself, managed to get up. Then she moved painfully across the living room floor, hobbling around the sleeping bodies, and went into the kitchen.

A woman was sitting in a rocking chair, holding

a sleeping baby. Both the baby and the woman looked very, very tired. Jennie asked, "Is it four in the morning or afternoon, please?"

"Morning," the woman said shortly.

"Then it will soon be light," Jennie said. She was still so much in a daze that she was really talking to herself, not the woman. She continued, "I have to find my brother and mother. Do you know if the flood waters came as high as Witten Street?"

"Higher," the woman answered. "I heard that most of the town is under water. Nearly everyone is dead."

Jennie moved toward the door of the kitchen. She was numb with pain and despair, but she was determined to find her family. And Jim Hurst. Had Jim rescued her last night or had she just dreamed it?

"You can't leave like that," the woman said.

"Like what?" Jennie asked.

"You're barefoot. And bleeding. And you've lost your dress."

Jennie looked down at her slip and for the first time she understood that the flood had actually pulled the dress right off of her body. "Never mind," she said. "When I find my house and my family, I'll put on my other dress."

"They're all dead," the woman pronounced. "You'd better go in there and rest till help comes. The men promised me they'd send help this morning."

"What men?"

"The Johnstown rescue squad," the woman explained. "They promised if I'd just let these people stay here one night, they'd find other places for them this morning."

"If there were men to organize a rescue squad, then not everyone is dead," Jennie said. Her foot hurt so bad that she wished she could just sit down for a few minutes. And she wished the woman would offer her something to eat. Somehow she could tell by the cross look in the woman's eyes that she wouldn't do that.

"You can't go wandering around in the middle of the night with no clothes on," the woman said again.

"Do you have a dress?" Jennie asked hesitantly.

"No. Is that locket gold?"

Jennie's hands flew to her neck. The gold locket she'd inherited from her father's mother was still clasped around her neck. How could a flood be strong enough to rip a dress from her body and leave a fragile chain like this one?

"I'll give you a blanket for the locket," the woman said.

"And food," Jennie answered. The flood had taught her that she must keep her wits about her to survive.

The exchange was quick, and the woman wouldn't look at Jennie as she handed her a hunk of cheese and a hard-boiled egg. Jennie wrapped the old, ragged quilt around her shoulders and staggered out the door on her wounded foot.

Once outside, Jennie had no real idea where to go or what to do. She limped out of the house, clutching the blanket as though it were a fur shawl, and started walking down toward the river again. She had no idea what she was going to do once she got there, but there were fires and lights, which signified that there were people moving around down there.

The pain slowed her progress greatly, and she had to stop every few steps and rest her foot. As she neared the bridge, she saw that the wall of refuse was still burning, and the horror of being trapped inside it came back to her.

She caught her breath in fear and sat down on a fallen log. She decided to wait there a few minutes and sat mesmerized, watching the bridge burn. Even from this distance she could hear screams and smell the stench of death.

Had Jim Hurst really rescued her? It didn't seem possible that he'd be in Johnstown at all. She decided that she'd imagined the whole thing, that it must have been some other young man, as nameless as the one who'd saved the baby, who had carried her to safety.

She sat quietly, reliving the last twenty-four hours and trying to understand that her life was irrevocably changed. She couldn't feel much of anything except pain in her foot and dread the news that was to follow. What if the woman in the Edwards' house was right and every one of her family was dead?

She shook her head and refused to believe it was possible. Then she tried to rise from the log, but she was in so much pain that she really couldn't move out into the darkness again. She sat on the log and waited till daylight broke. As the sky lightened, the sight of the destruction below her made her wish for darkness again.

Everywhere Jennie looked she saw people wandering around with frightened, dazed faces. Most seemed to be searching for their family and friends. Some were moving back and forth, trying to help other people. There were bands of children who wandered alone. Old people supported each other as they walked from group to group.

From time to time, the fire in the river would blaze forth with renewed energy, and people would turn toward it with horror. In the first light of dawn, the screams from the burning bridge grew softer and finally stopped.

From where Jennie sat, she could see a panorama of the flood area down by the bridge. Debris was backed up for a block or more and piled high in a crazy puzzle of houses, fences, railroad ties, and unidentified parts.

Jennie sighed and let the tears roll down her face as she watched the action below. She saw a wooden cart pull up to the edge of the muddy bank, and three men jumped out. The men worked quickly and efficiently, moving among the clusters of people and stopping now and then. When they stopped, they carried someone away and dumped them onto the wooden cart.

Jennie watched the operation for several minutes before she realized that they were carrying dead bodies. Where would they bury so many people? The graveyard was high enough up on a hill to have avoided the flood, but it was too small for so many bodies.

Jennie began to sob, and then she tried to stand up again. This time she spied a straight stick that she could use as a walking cane, and she used it to walk down the hill toward the other people. It was easier to move now that it was light and she had the stick.

She went first to the men who had the wooden cart of bodies and asked, "Have any of you seen Mrs. Brooks? Or my brother, Peter?"

They didn't even bother to answer, but one man shook his head, and she went on to the next group, asking the same question. Slowly, hobbling on her wounded foot, she walked from group to group, asking for news of her family. As she walked, she moved in the general direction of their boardinghouse.

She walked as instinctively as she had fought for life. Without any kind of conscious awareness of what she was doing, she put one foot in front of the other, moving in dogged determination to find her family.

From time to time she asked for news of Jim Hurst, and whenever she did, she chided herself for her foolishness. She had dreamed that Jim was in Johnstown, and there was no sense looking for him. She hardly dared to hope that he had survived the flood at all.

It was slow moving for Jennie, and she walked as though she were guided by someone else. As the pain in her leg grew worse, she began to believe that her father's ghost was guiding her. Then she imagined that she saw her mother and her brother just ahead of her.

Reality was blurred by such delirious hallucinations, but Jennie was propelled by a greater strength and courage than she had ever thought possible. Two days before, if anyone had told her that she would be walking down the street in a torn petticoat and ragged blanket, with a foot so sore that she could hardly bear to step on it, she would not have believed it. She didn't quite believe it now.

She moved toward their boardinghouse with no thought for herself, concerned only for her family. She wanted to see her mother and brother. She wanted to hold them in her arms, and to know that they were all right.

From time to time, a scene from the nightmare of the flood would flash across her mind, but she tried to keep her mind from going back to the sights and the sounds she had just lived through.

Home. She was propelled by the same survival instinct that saved her from drowning and caused her to rescue the little baby. She wanted to be oblivious to the screams of the dying and the cries of the lost and wounded people she passed. She didn't want to see the dazed faces of displaced people who were wandering beside her.

She turned the corner toward the boardinghouse, drawing closer to the banks of the flood. She stepped over a corpse, which she hadn't seen, just in time to avoid stumbling. She began to search the faces of the bodies that had washed onto shore in this neighborhood near her home.

Then she was standing at the end of her street, where her boardinghouse should have been, but all she saw was a pile of rubble where she thought the brick building should be standing.

All the houses in the neighborhood had collapsed and were unrecognizable. The whole street was a mass of twisted and warped building materials, none of which she recognized. The mud beneath her feet seemed to ooze destruction, and Jennie knew that she would dream about this despairing land-scape all of her life.

There simply was no boardinghouse. She began to recognize pieces of some of the rubble that sur-rounded her home, and she was dismayed to see the sign from the Johnstown Bank lying amidst the wreckage. The Johnstown Bank was a full mile up-stream from this location.

There was nothing to show that she and her fam-ily had ever lived there. She stood looking at the spot for quite a while, hoping to find any familiar object. She would have welcomed a vase or the rem-nants of a kitchen chair. Anything at all that would prove that they had once lived there would be some-thing. But it was gone, all gone.

Chapter Fourteen

FACING the obliteration of her home made Jennie even more exhausted and sick than she had been before. She stared for as long as she could bear to, and then she turned away and began to climb toward higher ground.

She had gone only a few feet when she tripped over a log and fell to the ground, where she collapsed in sobs. She lay there until she had sobbed her heart out and then sank into a light sleep.

Two young children, about nine or ten years old, found her lying on the ground. One of them called out, "Here's another dead one."

A third, older friend ran over and looked at her. She heard the friend say, "Naw, she's alive."

Jennie struggled to sit up as one of the younger

boys said, "You need some help, miss?" The three boys half-carried and half-dragged her up the hill to another house.

She protested, "I have to find my family," but they brought her inside the house anyway.

A woman met her in the living room and asked her to sit down in a rocking chair. There were other people in the room, but they didn't pay any attention to her. Most of them were lying on the floor or sitting with their backs against the walls. Some were talking in low voices, others simply stared straight ahead, seeing nothing.

"Have some tea," the woman offered and poured her some tea from a china teapot.

Jennie sipped the tea gratefully, cupping her hands around the fragile china cup as though she'd never seen anything so dainty before.

The woman who sat next to her was writing things down, and she asked Jennie her name and how old she was. Jennie watched as she wrote her name and age and address on a piece of white paper with a goose-quill pen.

"My name is Mrs. Whitaker," the woman said. "This is my home, and I've taken in as many refugees as I can. You can stay here as long as you like."

"I have to find my family," Jennie protested. Then she minded her manners by adding, "but thank you. That's very kind of you."

"This is a terrible disaster," Mrs. Whitaker said. "Families separated. Houses torn apart. I still can't believe it is as bad as they say. Impossible to believe that a thousand are dead."

"A thousand?" Jennie asked in horror. If a thousand people were killed, what chance did her family have?

"Were you with your family when the flood hit?" Mrs. Whitaker asked.

"No. I was in South Fork," Jennie answered.

The woman stared at her, and Jennie knew she didn't believe her. Jennie repeated, "I was in the telegraph tower in South Fork, and I rode the flood down here to Johnstown."

"My dear, South Fork is over ten miles away."

"Fourteen," Jennie corrected her. Mrs. Whitaker shook her head. "I was lucky because I held onto things, and I was never right in the middle of the flood. I was always on the edges."

"If you came from South Fork, your family would be in South Fork," Mrs. Whitaker said gently. She sounded as though she were talking to an invalid.

"No. My mother is here in Johnstown. I have to find her." Jennie could see that the woman wasn't believing anything she said. She tried to explain one more time, "I live in Johnstown, but I was visiting in South Fork. When the flood hit, I was washed down to Johnstown."

"Yes, dear. You'd better rest."

"I've already rested," Jennie said. "I have to find my mother. And my brother. Or my friend Jim. Or my friend Millie. Or *anyone* I know." Tears were rolling down her face.

"You need to have someone look at that foot," the woman said. "Can you stand on it?"

"I've walked all over Johnstown," Jennie said.

She rose to show the woman and immediately sank down again. The pain was dreadful.

"I'll give you something for the pain," the woman said. "Then I'll bandage your foot before you leave."

She handed Jennie a second cup of steaming tea, and this time she added a few drops of medicine to it. Jennie drank the tea without even asking what was in it. In seconds she dozed off, sitting in the rocking chair. The last thing she remembered was the woman patting her on the shoulder and saying, "You'll feel better soon."

She dreamed it was a summer day, and she was walking with her father through a meadow. Her mother and brother were sitting by the side of the road on a flat rock, and when they drew near, they began to wave. She and her father ran through the meadow toward her mother and brother. The sun was shining, and it was a perfectly beautiful day.

When she awoke someone was bending over her, washing her hurt foot with cold rags. She tried to draw her foot back, but the woman who held her was strong. She said, "I've cleaned the wound as well as I can. Now we have to find you a pair of shoes to keep that cut clean. The men from the rescue squad have brought a few extra clothes."

She handed Jennie a pair of men's black shoes, which were about two sizes too big. "These will have to do until you can take the bandage off," the woman said.

Jennie let the woman pull the big shoe over the bandaged foot and stared down as the woman tightened the laces. When the woman started to pull on the other one, Jennie said, "I'd rather leave the one foot barefoot. It will be easier to walk."

The woman nodded her head in agreement and said, "Now that your foot is bandaged, you'll be all right."

"Thank you," Jennie said. She wondered silently if she would ever be all right again. Memories of the flood seemed to keep washing over her in waves.

"Are you strong enough to help?" the woman asked.

"I need to find my family," Jennie said.

The woman said softly, "There's someone who knows you in the kitchen. I talked with her while you were sleeping, and she says you're telling the truth."

"Who is it?"

"Mrs. Marsh," the woman said. "She says she knew your family."

Jennie heard the word *knew*, and her heart caught in her throat. She jumped up and limped toward the kitchen. Once there, she saw her old neighbor, Mrs. Marsh, and threw her arms around her.

Mrs. Marsh kissed her on both cheeks and held her tight and said, "You look strong, Jennie. Can you help me with the cooking?"

Jennie shook her head and said, "I have to find my family."

"Child, you'll do better to stay here for a while. The rescue squad will round everyone up eventually. We're sending in our list of names in a few minutes."

Mrs. Whitaker added, "There are so many to feed and take care of. We need all the able-bodied help we can get. Can you help us here?" She reached out a hand and pulled Jennie toward the kitchen sink. Jennie felt dizzy, but she nodded her head and said, "Yes, I can help."

"Good," Mrs. Marsh said, "you can help make some soup. We're going to have to try to feed as many people as we can until real help comes."

"Will Mrs. Whitaker really turn my name in to the rescue squad?"

"Yes."

Jennie said, "I'll do what I can." Though she was still clothed in a petticoat, with Mrs. Edwards' blanket draped around her shoulders, Jennie hobbled over to the kitchen table and began helping Mrs. Marsh chop carrots and onions for the soup.

Chapter Fifteen

PEOPLE came in from time to time to get the large pots of soup off the stove and to pass out bowls to the people who congregated in the yard, hoping for anything to eat. Jennie chopped vegetables all that morning, but she realized the activity was futile. There was no way they could ever cook enough soup to feed the masses of people that were wandering around in a daze outside.

From time to time, strangers came into the kitchen, looking for their loved ones. They never found anyone they were looking for. About noon, Jennie heard a voice say, "Why, it's the boomer girl. I thought you must be dead!"

Jennie looked up from the raw carrots and saw the young reporter, David Winters, standing across the table. He had a pencil and a notebook in his hand. He was the only person Jennie had seen all day who didn't look tired. He was cheerful as he asked, "You remember me, don't you? We talked yesterday?"

Jennie nodded. He smiled broadly, "Say, I'm glad you're alive. Can you come with me?"

Jennie was startled at the question, and she stepped backward in surprise.

He said, "Some other reporters will be coming into town soon. As soon as they get here we will have to string telegraph wires and set up a station. Will you help us?"

Jennie had no idea what he was talking about. She managed to ask, "How did you get here?"

"By train," David answered. "Well, I started by train but I walked the last bit . . . say, you're in pretty bad condition. You need some rest."

"I had some rest," she said. To Jennie, David Winters appeared to be a magical being. He looked so young and so healthy and not the least bit fazed by what was going on outside. She said, "I've got to find my mother. Can you help me?"

"You won't find your mother standing around in your petticoat chopping vegetables," David pointed out reasonably.

Jennie blushed and stammered, "I can't go out. I'm not dressed properly."

"No, you're certainly not." David smiled at her and said, "This has been an exciting day for me. Not only have I got the scoop of the century but I get to see a pretty girl in her petticoat."

Jennie stepped back from the young reporter. She was embarrassed and so confused by the day's events that tears began to roll down her cheeks again.

David said, "Wait a minute, boomer girl. Don't cry."

Jennie didn't speak.

"I'll tell you what, I'll get you a dress if you'll come with me. I'm going to need a good boomer just as soon as we get the wires strung. How about it, is that a deal?"

Jennie nodded.

"What's your name?"

"Jennie."

David smiled again and said, "You wait right there. I'll be back in no time."

Jennie didn't really believe he would return at all. She went back to chopping vegetables because it was the only thing she could think to do. Mrs. Marsh, who was running the kitchen, gave the small bowls of soup to the people waiting outside. From time to time she offered Jennie a bowl. Jennie refused. She was still too numb and too grief-stricken to eat.

At one o'clock Mrs. Marsh said, "Eat the soup, girl, you're going to need it."

"I need a dress," Jennie ventured.

"I told the rescue squad you needed a dress," Mrs. Marsh said. "They say there are a lot of people in worse shape than you. But in an emergency you're all right in your petticoat." Mrs. Marsh frowned and added, "At least for the time being."

Jennie was still chopping onions when David came back in with a dark-green cotton dress, a pink sunbonnet, some black high-topped shoes, and a bright-red shawl. He handed them to her and asked anxiously, "Will these do?"

Jennie nodded her head and pulled the dress quickly over her head. She buttoned the high buttons up to her neck, and bent down to put the one shoe on her good foot. She was relieved to find that it was just her size. She said, "I'll save the other shoe till my foot heals. I don't know how to thank you."

He laughed at that and said, "Oh I know how you can thank me. I tell you I need a boomer as fast as possible."

"Where did you get the clothes?"

"Don't ask."

Jennie's heart sank as she realized she was probably wearing the clothes of a dead woman.

David said, "The other fellows will be coming in any time now, and I want to make sure that my story gets over the wires before anyone else's." He turned to Jennie, and his eyes were shining as he said, "This is the biggest scoop that any reporter has had since Lincoln was shot. Do you realize that?" Then he pulled back, stopped himself, and said, "Poor girl, of course you don't realize that, you're one of the victims. How's that foot doing? We ought to get you to the doctor."

But Jennie shook her head and said, "I've got to find my mother, my brother."

"But you promised me," David reminded her.

"I'll come as soon as I find them," Jennie said.

David shook his head doubtfully, "You haven't been outside. There are thousands of people milling around. You're in for a shock."

"I've got to find them," Jennie answered simply.

David shrugged his shoulders as though to say he might have known that she would put her family first, and he said, "Well, we won't have any telegraph poles until tonight anyway. Will you promise me that you will come to the brickyard tonight?"

Jennie said, "I'll come as soon as I can find my family."

David said, "I'm on my way to an organizational meeting at the Town Hall. Do you want to come with me?"

"A meeting?"

"It's a meeting of the rescue squad at one o'clock today. An organizational meeting till other help comes. You might see your mother or brother there," David suggested. "Can I escort you?"

He held his arm out to steady her. Dressed in the dark-green dress, Jennie stepped out of the house and onto the muddy path. David escorted her down toward the center of Johnstown. For the first time since the flood, Jennie felt almost normal as she walked toward the Presbyterian Church.

It was less a dream than a nightmare. They passed hundreds of people who were walking around in a daze. Some of them were limping badly. They passed dead bodies; they also passed the bodies of dead animals bloated and already decaying.

David said, "It's beginning to smell. It will be a lot worse by tomorrow."

Jennie shuddered at his callousness but said nothing. She held onto his arm as they made their way toward the meeting.

The meeting was held in the sanctuary of the church and there were at least two hundred people there. Jennie took a seat in the back so she could look at everyone, but David went right up front so he could hear the speakers.

All of them spoke about the need for order and discipline, but they didn't seem very orderly or disciplined themselves. They quarreled quite a bit.

One man said that he wanted armed police at every corner before sunset. No one bothered to ask him where the police were to come from. Most of the suggestions were so foolish that they were promptly rejected, but within thirty minutes John Mocksom had been elected leader of Johnstown, and he was handing out jobs.

Someone had cut tin stars out of tomato can ends. He passed the stars out to those who would be burying the dead, telling people exactly what to do. Temporary morgues were set up, one in the Episcopal church, another in the only remaining bank in town.

Jennie sat in the back of the room, listening to the activities with blurred interest. She quickly realized that the meeting was nearly all men and that the chances that her mother and young brother would be there were very small. She was impressed that these men thought enough about the public welfare that they were determined to restore order. But as for herself, she was ready to go outside and start looking for her mother again.

About fifteen minutes after the meeting began, David was writing furiously, taking notes; Jennie stood up and started toward the door when she saw Jim Hurst walk in. Jim was as astounded to see her as she was to see him. His face turned white as he said, "Jennie! Where have you been? I've been looking all over for you."

Jim's face suddenly seemed to grow dim and hazy. Then Jennie felt herself falling. When she woke a few minutes later, Jim and David were both standing over her.

"You fainted," said David, and began telling Jim where he found her. "I'm going to need her for a boomer, you know. We'll have the wires strung, maybe later today."

Jim looked at him and frowned and said, "Jennie can't do anything until she gets her foot taken care of."

Jennie realized that Jim had taken the shoe off her foot and was looking at it. He asked, "Did anyone clean this?"

"Yes."

"With antiseptic?"

Jennie wasn't sure. She shrugged. She felt very faint and tired, but she was glad to see Jim. She reached out and touched his face. Jim picked her up and carried her out of the meeting hall, down the steps, and across the muddy street to another building where he set her down on the porch and said, "Wait here."

He came back a few minutes later, and saying, "The doctors are too busy, but I got some antiseptic for your foot." He carried a small bottle of antiseptic and a rag. Kneeling in front of her, he asked, "Jennie, are you brave?"

Jennie was still numb from the day's events. She didn't bother to answer a question that seemed so foolish.

Jim said, "Take a deep breath and try not to scream." Then he poured the antiseptic onto the cloth to begin cleaning the wound on her foot. He worked quickly and efficiently, but the wound was open and still bleeding. Jennie choked off a scream by biting her lip.

Jim said, "Don't faint again. I've had a long day, and I don't want to carry you anymore. This is the second time today, you know."

"I'm sorry," Jennie said. Tears rolled down her cheeks.

"Don't be sorry, Jennie! It was supposed to be a joke. You're a brave person."

"You really did rescue me from the bridge, didn't you?"

"Yes. I came back to look for you, but you were already gone. Jennie, did you really ride the flood all the way from South Fork?"

Jennie couldn't stop the tears, "Oh, Jim, it was so awful. I can't tell you how awful it was."

"You'll have to tell someone eventually," Jim said,

"you can't keep it bottled up inside of you."

"Aunt Nettie and Aunt Hester must both be dead," Jennie said. "The water came up over the telegraph office. I never would have believed that it would come so high."

"They're saying that in parts of the gorge it went up the banks over two hundred feet," Jim answered gravely.

"How could it go so high, Jim? What happened?"

Jim shook his head and said, "I don't understand all of it, of course, but where the valley narrows the water had to splash up the sides of the gorge, and then having all of the debris rushing along made the water go even higher. That's why it caused so much destruction."

Jennie nodded. It was good to be talking to someone she knew, and it was good to begin to think a little again. She asked, "Where were you when the flood hit?"

Jim laughed and asked her, "Didn't David tell you? We were both on the train. I was trying to warn people on the train. David helped me."

"David?"

"You know, the reporter that you were with."

"Oh."

Jim saw that none of this was making much sense to her. "Have you had any food?"

"No," Jennie answered. "I don't want to eat, I just want to find my mother."

Jim said, "Your mother is in Alma Hall with my mother."

"Are you just telling me that?"

"No, it's true," Jim answered. "Your mother, and my mother, and a whole lot of other people spent the night in Alma Hall. I was there just an hour ago. I saw your mother, and she and your brother are just fine."

Jennie struggled to her feet, wrapped the cloak around her, and started to limp toward Alma Hall. Jim caught her arm. "You can't get in, it's all blocked off. They're full up — in fact, they're trying to move people out to relatives on higher ground."

"Aunt Hester and Aunt Nettie lived on high ground," Jennie sobbed. "I need to see my mother."

Jim said, "Let me find you a place to rest, Jennie. Tomorrow I'll take you to Alma Hall. I have to go to the church and work in the morgue."

"I don't want to rest. I'm not tired, it's still daytime," Jennie answered. "*I need to see my mother!*"

Jim sighed and said, "Well, there is plenty of work to be done, I guess it won't matter if I'm a little bit late. I'll go with you."

Jim and Jennie picked their way through the ruins of Johnstown. As they moved through the streets it seemed more like a desolate battlefield than a town. People still wandered to and fro, dead animals lay in the middle of the streets, houses were turned up on their sides or lay in pieces on the ground. Above all, there was mud. The smell of the burning bridge in the distance kept everyone on edge.

As they walked, Jennie looked toward the fire and said, "I almost burned to death. Thank you for rescuing me."

Jim put his arm around her and asked again, "Did

you really ride the water all the way from South Fork?"

Jennie nodded her head and the tears began to stream down her face again. She said, "Yes, though I can't remember very well."

Jim squeezed her arm and said, "You'll remember better after a while. You're tired now, and this was a terrible ordeal. Right now you need something to eat and to sleep."

Jennie stopped and looked at Jim. "How can you talk about eating and sleeping with all this going on around you?" she said.

Jim answered gravely, "Those of us who are alive need to stay healthy to help those who are dead. If we don't get the dead buried quickly we will have a disaster much worse than the flood on our hands."

"You mean because the bodies smell?" Jennie asked.

"Yes," Jim answered quietly, "but more because of typhoid. You know unsanitary conditions bring typhoid and other illnesses. If it sweeps through Johnstown we could all die."

"I've heard of that. In my grandmother's day, there were whole towns that died from typhoid."

"You don't want that to happen, do you Jennie?"

"Are you telling me that if I eat something, Johnstown won't get typhoid?" Jennie looked furious.

Jim looked a little angry himself, and then he put both his hands on her shoulders and shook her lightly and said, "Jennie, it's foolish to quarrel. Let's be glad we're alive. I'm so glad I found you."

Jennie didn't answer but she knew in her heart

that Jim was right. She followed him quietly through the debris, picking her way over things, trying not to see what was all around her. Trying not to hear the sobs of people who were walking along the paths with her and trying just to keep her mind on what was in front of her.

It was a long, arduous walk to Alma Hall. As they found their way through the streets, Jennie took Jim's hand and said, "I've lived in Johnstown all my life, and I don't even know where I am. What street is this?"

Jim stopped and looked around him. "I believe it's South Main."

"But look at the bank over there," Jennie pointed to a shambles of bricks and a sign that said JOHNS-TOWN BANK.

"I think the bank was swept down the road," Jim answered. "Don't worry about it, we'll get it all sorted out one of these days."

"Oh, yes, the age of progress," Jennie sneered. And then she said, "I'm sorry, Jim, you've been kind to me. I'll try not to quarrel."

Jim smiled and hugged her close to him. "You're alive, that's all that matters. I don't care if you have a temper. It's a sign of life."

Then they had reached Alma Hall. They waded through the muddy waters, Jim first, and then Jennie knocked on the door. Someone opened the door a crack and peeked out.

Jim asked, "We've come to see Mrs. Brooks and her son. Are they still here?"

A weary voice answered, "Yes, but we can't take any more people."

"This is Mrs. Brooks' daughter," Jim answered.

"We can't take any more people," the voice repeated. "We're full up."

"I just want to see my mother," Jennie pleaded. "Please!"

The door opened another crack, and a man's voice said, "You're Burt Brooks' daughter?"

"Yes, I am."

"Come in."

Jennie didn't know the man, but she assumed that whoever he was, he had worked for her father at one time, and she was grateful that her father's name was the password to get her inside Alma Hall.

Jim gently touched her arm and then left her to go inside the hotel.

Chapter
Sixteen

JOHNSTOWN   JUNE 1   3:15 P.M.

ALMA Hall was the fanciest hotel in town. Although Jennie had only been there a few times, she was shocked to remember what it had been like, and to see what it had become. There were no more velvet chairs or fancy, embossed wallpaper. Everything was different from before.

Only twenty-four hours ago she had been talking to David and dreaming about a life of travel and adventure. Now she had all the adventure that anyone could hope for. But it was not the adventure dreams were made of.

She walked through the once-fancy lobby, up the stairs, and started going from room to room, searching out the faces until she found her mother and her brother, Peter, on the third floor.

Her mother looked relatively rested and re-freshed, and when she saw Jennie she screamed in surprise, jumped up, and ran and threw her arms around her daughter, hugging her tightly, so tightly that Jennie could hardly breathe.

Her mother had obviously thought Jennie was dead. She held onto Jennie and began pouring out the story of their night in Alma Hall, saying, "There weren't any candles and after a while there was no water. There was something to eat, though. We formed a police patrol with Reverend Beal, who was in charge of it all. We sang hymns most of the night. I was so grateful to get here.

"Oh Jennie, our boardinghouses are gone, totally demolished! We'll have to start all over again, won't we?"

"Yes," Jennie answered. Her heart sank at the years of work and labor that she and her mother had put into the boardinghouses. All gone in a flash of an eye.

Her mother must have been thinking the same thing because she began to sob and said, "Oh, I'm not as young as I used to be. I won't be able to do it all over. I haven't the energy. I haven't the strength."

Jennie walked with her mother over to a chair in the corner and put her arm around her and tried to soothe her. "There, there. I have a job starting this evening. I'm going to be a telegraph operator for a reporter. I'm sure he'll pay me well. He seems to have a lot of money."

That did seem to cheer her mother up somewhat,

and eventually she got quieter. They talked for a bit about Aunt Hester and Aunt Nettie, speculating on whether or not they might have survived the flood.

Her brother, Peter, who had been waiting silently beside their mother, then began to ask Jennie questions about what had happened to her.

Jennie told her brother and her mother all about having the water knock down the telegraph tower and she told as much about her trip down the river as she could remember, but there was very little of it she remembered at all.

Then, as she was telling it, she remembered the baby that she had saved, and she said to her brother, "I saved a baby's life."

"You did?" He sighed wistfully and said, "I thought we were having an adventure, but you're a real heroine, aren't you, Jennie?"

"There will be many heroines and heroes today," Jennie predicted. She thought about the men who had met in the Town Hall, and she said, "I went with the reporter I met to a Town Hall meeting, and Mr. Melrose was there. His whole family had been killed, but he was there supervising the grave-digging. That's a different kind of hero — it's a real hero to be able to do that. Don't you think?"

"Yes, I do," her mother answered promptly. They talked for a while longer and then her mother said, "We have some bread and cheese we can share with you, dear. Have you had anything to eat in the last twenty-four hours?"

"No," Jennie admitted.

Her mother whispered to her to come over, and she brought out a small block of cheese and a small hunk of bread and said to Jennie, "I'll stand in front of you and you can eat as quietly as possible. We're running out of food here, you know. But everyone inside the Hall had the same rations to begin with."

"Mother made me save mine," Peter said. "And I haven't been very hungry at all. You can have some of mine, too, Jennie."

"No, I won't take either of yours, it isn't fair," Jennie answered.

But in the end she ate all of her brother's bread and all of the remaining cheese and bread that her mother had, declaring it was the best food she had ever eaten in her life. They had a space in the corner of one of the hotel rooms. Her mother insisted on examining the wound on Jennie's foot. She looked at it anxiously and said Jennie should try to keep it as clean as possible.

At four-thirty, a gentleman knocked on the door and announced that there would be no supper. He said, "People are free to leave or stay as they wish. There aren't any more rations to be handed out."

Several people began to complain, and the man who brought the news said, "We're hoping for supplies by tomorrow."

Jennie suggested that they might try to move on to one of the other shelters. She described in loving detail the vegetable soup that Mrs. Marsh was giving away. They also talked of going to higher ground or to one of the other villages. In the end they decided that the best thing would be for them to spend one more night in Alma Hall and then try to make better arrangements the next day.

"I must go back," Jennie said, "the reporter has promised me a job."

"Not until morning," her mother said. They debated for a while but her mother won the argument, declaring, "No self-respecting young lady would go out on this night."

Peter seemed very anxious about going to sleep, and he crawled up close to Jennie and whispered in her ear, "Do you believe in ghosts?"

Jennie said, "I'm not sure. Maybe."

Peter said, "There must be hundreds of ghosts around here."

Jennie said, "Hush, go to sleep." She was entirely too tired and too numb from the day's events to worry about anything as abstract as ghosts.

Chapter Seventeen

JENNIE woke at four o'clock the next morning, and she sat straight up and stared into the darkness. She was awake for a few minutes before she realized that she had not been dreaming. Terrible things had happened to her. Her foot was throbbing, really throbbing with pain, and she realized that pain had awakened her.

She sat in the dark, huddled in the shawl that David Winter had found for her. She thought first about David, trying to imagine what kind of person he really was. He had seemed excited — almost happy in the midst of such great tragedy. Was it possible that he was totally unfeeling? She understood that he had no relatives here in Johnstown, but was it possible that a reporter could train himself to be as nerves-of-steel as David seemed to be?

Then her thoughts turned to Jim Hurst. He had grown up in Johnstown, and he was obviously shaken by the events. How concerned and how worried Jim had looked! In a way, he was the opposite of David. Yet Jim had chosen to work for the men who caused the tragedy. She shivered as she realized that no matter how kind Jim himself was, he was a member of the enemy camp.

She drew the shawl tighter around her and tried to think what was best to do now. How would they manage? If her foot were better, she would have attempted to hike out of Johnstown and up into the hills. They had friends in one of the smaller villages who would take them in. But with her bad foot, it didn't seem practical even to try. Help would surely come in a day or two. As soon as the telegraph wires were strung, word would get out to the rest of the world, and help would come. She wondered if the telegraph wires were strung yet. If they were, the most sensible thing that she could do would be to try and get the job that David had offered her. If they had money it would help.

She sat worrying in the cold, gloomy morning. Eventually the sky got lighter, and her mother stirred on the pallet beside her. Mrs. Brooks stretched her arms, looked at her daughter and smiled. She patted her cheek and said, "Jennie, no matter what comes after this, I'll be happy. I thought you were dead, my dear."

"Aunt Nettie and Aunt Hester probably are," Jennie said.

Her mother nodded and said, "I know that is possible, but we must never give up hope. Perhaps they will come riding down the valley as you did."

Privately, Jennie doubted that was going to happen, but if it helped her mother to believe it, it was fine with her. Her mother sighed again and looked at her young son and she said quietly, "I'm glad you knew your father, Jennie. I think it has been important for you. I only wish that Peter had stronger memories of him. He was a fine man, wasn't he?"

"Yes, mother." Jennie told her how the magic of her father's name had helped her gain admittance to Alma Hall.

Her mother was very pleased with the story, and she said, "We should be grateful that we're all together and that we have a roof over our heads."

At six, when the light was a little stronger, Jennie walked to the window and looked out. Her mother stood by her side, and they looked out at the burning pile of debris. The fire still smoldered, and Jennie said quietly, "I almost burned to death."

Her mother answered, "I have heard that the screams of the people who were burning to death traveled all over the valley. It was one reason why I didn't leave Alma Hall. The walls not only protected us from the rain, they protected us from the truth. Oh, Jennie, I can hardly bear to think of starting over. Where will we go? What will we do?"

Jennie put her arm around her mother and said, "I think that the best thing is for you and Peter to stay here at Alma Hall and let me go and, if I can, arrange for some kind of housing for all of us."

"We still have money in the bank," her mother said. "A hundred and sixty-three dollars."

"Mother, that bank was buried under ten feet of mud when I walked by it yesterday," Jennie said. "It will be a long time before you get your money out, if ever."

"What will we do, how will we eat?" her mother whispered.

"Don't despair, help will come." Jennie tried to make her voice sound grown up. "Right now I must go and see if there was any truth in the employment offer that Mr. Winters made me."

She combed her curly hair as best she could with her fingers and wished that there was some way to brush her teeth and wash her face. But the little water that was available had to be boiled, and it was all for drinking. Jennie knew that the unspoken fear of all the survivors was typhoid. Boiling water was a simple precaution, but germs could spread in any number of ways. The most prevalent one was decaying corpses.

Jennie frowned down at her feet. She was still wearing the big black boot on her wounded foot and the small brown boot on the other one. It made it difficult to walk. Limping, hungry, and light-headed, she climbed the hill toward the brickyard where David said they would set up the telegraph office.

When she got there she knocked loudly on the door. No one answered. Disappointed, Jennie decided to sit down and wait. Then she thought she heard some noises from around back. She went around the back, wading through the ever-present mud, and found some workmen stringing wire. One of them was very high on the telephone pole.

David Winters stood with a group of workmen on the ground. He looked over at her and said, "Oh, there you are, boomer girl. We'll be ready to go in about an hour, I would say. I hope you're fit to work hard?"

"Not without food," Jennie answered boldly. "I need food for myself and money for my family."

David nodded and reached into his pocket, pulling out a silver dollar. He handed it to Jennie and said, "Buy food then, and eat a good breakfast. I want you back here in one hour. With any luck, I'll get my story out before the others come."

Jennie took the silver dollar and looked at it, staring hard, and then asked, "But where shall I get food?"

"There are some farmers down at the corner who are selling food."

Jennie walked toward the center of town, where she was able to buy three hard-boiled eggs and a hunk of cheese from a farmer in a wagon. It cost her the whole dollar. Very carefully, she carried the food back to Alma Hall. She gave most of the cheese and two eggs to her mother, saying, "Now don't give this to anyone except Peter. Eat the food, and I'm going to work. I'll be at the brickyard. As soon as possible, I'll try to arrange better lodgings for you."

Her mother seemed weaker, frailer, and older today than she had the day before. She nodded her head, and then she looked anxiously over at her young son, who was still sleeping, and said, "Do you think I should let him sleep all morning?"

"Let him sleep as long as he can," Jennie answered. "And don't worry about him. He's a young, healthy, strong boy. His powers of recuperation are great."

"How's your foot?" her mother asked. "No puffiness, or redness, or swelling?"

"No, no, my foot is healing," Jennie answered impatiently. Privately she wondered if that were really the case. The foot seemed more sore, more swollen than ever to her. But there was no sense telling her mother. She tried to walk as straight as she could as she left Alma Hall so that her mother would not see how much she was limping.

She went quickly back to the brickyard. Going around to the back, and seeing that the wires were still not strung, she stood quietly waiting for David to speak to her. Finally he turned to her and he said, "Well, you might as well go inside and get some rest. I'll wake you when this is done."

"I'm not sleepy."

"You'll be tired later," David said. "Go inside and get some rest."

Jennie went inside. She found a huge room and wondered how in the world they would ever make a telegraph office out of it. Then, to her dismay, she saw that there were two telegraph Morse code machines there and a couple of desks. She picked the desk closest to the window and sat down in a swivel chair, and within ten minutes she was fast asleep with her head on the desk. An hour later David came in, tapped her on the shoulder and asked, "Are you ready to go to work?"

"Are the wires up?" Jennie asked.

He answered, "I think so."

Jennie sat up straight and began tap, tap, tapping on the Morse code, and within seconds she got an answer back from Pittsburgh.

PITTSBURGH HERE, WHAT NEWS OF JOHNSTOWN?

Jennie turned and said, "They want news from Johnstown."

David smiled broadly and clamped his hand on her shoulder and said, "Well then, my girl, we'll give them the news of Johnstown. Work as fast as you can." He took out his small notebook and said, "To the *Philadelphia Enquirer*, from David Winters, Johnstown, PA. Destruction struck this mighty city yesterday. It's as though the earth opened up and swallowed half the citizens."

Jennie took three separate stories in dictation from David in the next two hours. He seemed to be filled with inexhaustible energy and great joy. He paced up and down the room dictating. Then three other reporters walked in.

David knew one of them. As he shook his hand, he said, "I knew you'd be here eventually. How did you get here?"

The man laughed and said, "I took the train to New York and then back up and around and in. Charlie here walked over the mountains."

Charlie said, "Yes, I came thirty-eight miles, and it took me twenty-four hours. He came five hundred miles in twelve hours. How's that for progress?"

The reporters flung their suitcases over in one corner. One of them lit a cigar, and the other one looked around the brickyard approvingly and said, "You've got a good setup here, Winters, pretty good for a cub reporter."

David pretended to be insulted and said, "Cub reporter, indeed! You're looking at the future star reporter for the *New York Times*. Oh, boy, what a scoop this has been. What a scoop!"

"I hope you didn't do the whole story single-handedly," Burt said.

"There is plenty to write about," David assured him. "But you have to face the fact that my stories will be in today's newspapers all alone. You'll have to wait for tomorrow's editions."

"Where did you find the boomer?" Charlie asked.

David went over to Jennie's desk and said, "Her name is Jennie; she rode down from South Fork on the water." Then he turned and said, "Say, Jennie, I want to interview you. You'll make a swell story."

"Not now," Charlie answered. "I want to put her to work. I've got a heck of a story to tell my readers."

So Jennie had to sit down again and immediately go to work tapping out the long story sent to the *Philadelphia Express* by Charlie. No sooner had she finished, than David wanted to send out another story. Burt objected and said that it was his turn. David said, "She's my boomer. I'm the one who's paying her."

At that Jennie stood up, turned around, and said,

"Let's get this straight. One, I am not a boomer, my name is Jennie Brooks. You may call me Miss Brooks. Two, I am very hungry, and I expect to be fed three meals a day. And three, I have to get my family safe and settled before I can continue to work in this position. I need money, and I need a good place for them. Now if you want me you will help me find these things."

The three men looked at her. The one who smoked a cigar was the first to speak, saying, "Right, that sounds good to me. How about five dollars a week for your pay?"

Jennie nodded, fearful she would give away how great her pleasure was at the enormous amount of money that they were offering her. Then the man added, "And your folks, they need a place to live? Have you got any relatives in the country? Maybe we can send them out there?"

"No, I don't think so. We may still have friends in Charlotte, though. I'm not sure."

"Well, we'll find something for them tomorrow," the man promised. "They're safe where they are, aren't they?"

"I suppose so," Jennie said doubtfully.

"I'll send some food over," David promised.

"When?" Jennie asked.

"At supper time," David said.

"They've missed lunch," Jennie insisted, "and so have I. I'd like some food now."

"Well, that's easy," said the big man, "that's what I brought in my knapsack: food. I've got a tin of meat I thought we could share for dinner, and some sugar and flour, and I brought in several provisions. Suppose I send this meat over to your mom, would that do it for the time being?"

Jennie agreed that it would. She told the man how to get to Alma Hall, and then she went back to tapping out the news story on the lines. By the time she had finished that story, three other reporters had arrived.

Jennie worked at the telegraph office until midnight that night, tapping out story after story of the Johnstown flood. Each of the stories was more horrendous than the next; but to Jennie, the words were just a blur. From time to time one of the stories would have some special significance for her, and she would realize that she was writing about someone she knew or about a building that she had once worked in. It was almost better not to know.

At midnight, David offered to walk her back to Alma Hall so she could get some sleep. On the walk home, David talked nonstop about how thrilled he was to have the "scoop of the century." Jennie was too tired even to be bothered by his bragging.

Her mother woke when she came in and offered her some of the tinned meat. Jennie shook her head and said, "No, save it for tomorrow. They are feeding me."

"I'm so proud of you." Her mother hugged her. "Jennie, I'm sorry that I ever objected to you learning to be a telegraph operator."

Jennie was pleased with her mother's praise, but all she said was, "I have to be back there at six o'clock. Promise to wake me."

Chapter Eighteen

JENNIE was on the job at six the next morning, but by the time she got there, four new reporters were waiting anxiously. The men quickly devised a system for sharing her services. Someone found an hourglass, and they took turns. They had fifteen minutes each for their turn, and every three hours Jennie got a twenty-minute break.

Jennie worked from six in the morning until twelve o'clock that night. The stories of the disaster poured through her fingers to the telegraph keys, through the wires and into the homes of the readers in New York, Philadelphia, Pittsburgh, Atlanta, and all over the world.

That evening a relief train arrived from Pittsburgh, and one of the reporters managed to locate a large hunk of ham and quite a few other provisions. Jennie was never hungry from that point on. However there were many people in the city of Johnstown who were *very* hungry. Some of them came to the door to beg from time to time. It broke Jennie's heart to see how badly so many people had been hit by the disaster.

Jennie's mother and brother stayed at Alma Hall until the second relief train brought five hundred tents. One of the reporters managed to get a tent for Jennie and her family, and a group of four reporters carried it up the side of a hill for Mrs. Brooks. They constructed a temporary dwelling, and it was a big relief to be out in the open air. It was a longer walk for Jennie back and forth to work, but it was much more pleasant being up on the side of the hill with the survivors.

The town of Johnstown, by this time, had developed a horrendous stench, a stench that no one talked about because it was so bad. Jennie trained herself not to notice.

Though Jennie worked from sunrise until midnight, and was unable to see much of anything that went on, she was at the center of the communications network for Johnstown, so she knew more about what was happening than probably anyone in the city.

For the first week she was the only telegraph operator, and then, as the hoard of reporters increased sharply, two other boomers joined them. Three desks were set up, and three telegraph operators were kept busy full-time.

The stories that flew through Jennie's fingertips were primarily about the disaster itself in the first few days. The estimates of the number of dead started at ten thousand and gradually worked their way down to twenty-two hundred.

Jennie recorded all the major events, but it seemed to her they were happening somewhere else. When the first relief train from Pittsburgh arrived, Jennie did not see it, but she tapped out the whole story several times as each reporter tried to retell the dramatic story of food and clothing for the homeless in a unique way. It seemed to Jennie that the reporters were holding a contest between themselves to see who could describe the scenes most vividly.

David was the fastest thinker. Stories rolled off his tongue with an ease that amazed Jennie. She could hardly keep up with him. And she noticed that David's stories were often about people rather than events.

Some of the stories during the first three days described the scene of the disaster so vividly that Jennie felt sick sending the messages over the wire. She didn't really want to think about the decaying corpses, mass burials, or dismembered children that the reporters seemed to enjoy talking about.

Jennie fell into a heavy sleep as soon as she got home from work every night. She had only six hours before she had to get back to the brickyard and sit down in the swivel chair again. She did not dream, or if she did, she forgot her dreams before morning.

Jennie's life was soon swallowed up in the rigorous routine of tapping out the reporters' stories. She began to notice which reporters stuck to the facts of the story, and which ones were interested only in sensationalizing.

Sometimes the stories mentioned people that she knew or had known. Those were the hardest to send out to the newspapers and not take personally. One day David Winters did a whole story on her friend Willie Murphy's wild ride from the railroad station in South Fork into Johnstown. As he got to the part where the flood overtook Willie and derailed his train, Jennie burst into tears.

"Don't cry, Jennie. I'm sorry." David patted her on the back and said, "You're tired. We'll quit for a while."

"No. It's just that Willie was a friend of mine. I knew his wife and children, too. Now they're all dead." After saying that, Jennie began to think of her aunt Nettie and aunt Hester, and she really did break down and start to sob again.

David seemed very upset by her tears and called out to one of the other reporters, "Go get Jennie a cup of tea or something." He patted Jennie on the back, trying to soothe her.

Soon Jennie had a cup of tea and four solicitous reporters standing around her desk. She drank the tea as quickly as she could and got back to her work. Biting her lip to keep from crying, she tapped out the remainder of David's story. When it was over, he said, "At least your friend will go down in history. We've made him a hero, haven't we?"

"He made himself a hero," Jennie corrected. "All we did was tell the world about it."

"That's important, too," David said rather defensively.

Jennie didn't have the energy to argue with him, but she wasn't sure that all the stories going out over the wires were really doing anyone any good.

On the first Sunday after the flood, tourists poured in from all around the eastern part of the United States. Some of them brought picnic lunches and came simply to gawk. Others brought food for the hungry; some tried to sell it.

By the end of the first week there were a great many strangers in town, and many of them were no help at all. One man, who called himself Louis the Light, stood on street corners and made speeches. He also passed out pamphlets that said, *Whoops, whoops! We're all in the soup!*

Jennie didn't get a chance to see much of the town, but from time to time she walked through the streets and surveyed the progress. There was so much to clean up that at the beginning it was impossible to see whether anything had been accomplished.

People poured in from every corner of the nation, and most able-bodied people in Johnstown worked sixteen or twenty-hour days.

Jennie knew that Jim Hurst was working twenty-hour days at the morgue and grave sites, supervising the burials. From the newspaper reporters' stories, she knew that the makeshift morgues were still full of unidentified bodies. Many people were buried without anyone claiming them at all.

New bodies were discovered all the time. One morning Jennie was on her way to work when she saw a cart being pulled by an old woman. The body of a young child was on the cart, and the old woman struggled as she pulled it toward the morgue.

Jennie stopped to help the woman pull and was dismayed to recognize her old neighbor, Mrs. Ramsey. It seemed as though Mrs. Ramsey had aged twenty years in the last week. All Jennie could see was the child's muddy legs sticking out of the wagon. She was fearful that the child on the cart was one of Mrs. Ramsey's grandchildren but she didn't dare ask.

"You remember me, don't you?" Jennie asked as she took the lead in the pulling. "I'm Jennie Brooks."

"Oh, yes," Mrs. Ramsey said vaguely.

Jennie was never sure whether or not Mrs. Ramsey really knew who she was. She waited while the old woman went into the morgue and was surprised when Jim Hurst came out with her.

"Jennie!" he said. "I thought you would be working."

"I'm on my way to work," Jennie answered. Jim looked very tired and a lot older than his years. She wondered if her appearance had also changed drastically. The thought bothered her.

Jim took the wagon from Mrs. Ramsey and asked careful questions about how the child had died. Jennie was relieved to hear that it was not one of Mrs.

Ramsey's grandchildren at all. Jennie knew that the body must be one of the hundreds of bodies that were continuing to surface each day.

She heard Mrs. Ramsey telling Jim how the child's body had appeared in her cellar as the flood waters receded. "We don't know where the poor thing came from," Mrs. Ramsey said.

The reporters Jennie worked for had filed several stories about the morgue, and Jennie had trained herself not to get too upset by anything she heard, but she was sickened by the thought of that young life cut off so early.

Jim quickly took down Mrs. Ramsey's story and then he turned to Jennie and said, "I'd like to walk you to work but I haven't time."

"None of us have time for anything," Jennie said. She was suddenly aware of how rumpled and worn-out she must look. Did Jim even see her? He looked so tired and preoccupied that she doubted it.

"Any news of your aunts?" he asked.

She shook her head sadly.

"Don't give up. Every day there is a new miracle," Jim said.

"Now that the age of progress has failed, you're relying on miracles," Jennie snapped.

Jim said nothing at all but turned his back to her and went into the morgue. Jennie walked to work with a heavy heart. Why had she tried to pick a fight with Jim again? Why couldn't she let bygones be bygones?

Chapter Nineteen

W_{HEN} Jennie got to work that morning she
found several reporters standing around in a circle
as though they were looking at something very special. As she got closer to her desk, she realized that
the men were surrounding a small, elderly woman
in a dark-colored dress.

David Winters walked over to Jennie and leaned
his head toward her, whispering, "It's Clara
Barton."

Jennie was amazed that the famous little woman
who headed the American Red Cross would actually
bother to come into the newspaper office. She was
also delighted at the opportunity to get a look at
Miss Barton.

Since Clara Barton had come to town three days

before with her trainload of doctors and medical equipment, Jennie had sent out several stories describing Miss Barton's work. She knew that the little woman was sixty-seven years old and had been doing emergency nursing since the Civil War. She also knew that Clara Barton was a strong-minded woman who managed her Red Cross company with a very firm hand.

Jennie was curious about Clara Barton and awe-struck at the same time. She curtsied when she was introduced to the older woman and said, "Glad to meet you."

"What a pretty young girl," Clara Barton said crisply. She sounded surprised. The older woman reached up and touched Jennie's curling red hair. She spoke briskly and to the point, "Pretty."

"I found her in South Fork," David Winters said proudly.

Jennie hated the manner in which he claimed credit for her presence. It made her sound like a piece of property.

"South Fork," Miss Barton repeated. "Your home?"

"No, ma'am," Jennie replied. "I'm from Johnstown."

"And you can use the Morse code," Miss Barton said in an admiring manner.

It made Jennie quite shy to have Miss Clara Barton admire her skills. She blushed and said, "I can do little compared to someone like yourself."

"Ah, yes," Clara Barton almost snapped her reply, she was in such a hurry to do away with the pleasantries. It seemed that she agreed with Jennie about her own skills and didn't want to waste any time before she got back to work.

"Jennie rode the flood all the way from South Fork," David said. He seemed determined to show Jennie off as though she were his prize.

"That's nice." Clara Barton had obviously lost interest in Jennie.

"Well, to business, child," Clara Barton said. "I've come to send a telegram."

Jennie was surprised that the reporters had agreed to let Miss Barton use their telegraph office. Up until then, they'd been very firm that this office was for the use of the reporters only. But she suspected that Miss Barton was accustomed to getting special privileges quite often.

The telegram that Jennie typed out for Miss Barton was a simple demand for money from the American people. She listed the needs of the American Red Cross, and she also listed some of the ways the money would be spent. As she finished, she corrected herself and said, "Add boardinghouses. I intend to set up as many boardinghouses as possible for the homeless."

Jennie tapped out the request for boardinghouse funds. Then Miss Barton, who almost seemed to be talking to herself, said, "I have no idea who will run them, but I'll find someone."

"My mother," Jennie said promptly. "My mother can run your boardinghouses. We had two before the flood."

Miss Barton didn't seem surprised to find a solution so near at hand. She simply nodded her head and said, "Send your mother to me this afternoon. What's her name?"

"Brooks," Jennie answered, and Miss Barton swept from the room, walking as swiftly as she talked.

Once Miss Barton left the room, Jennie fell back into the routine of her work. She tapped out story after story, only half-thinking about what they said. When it was David's turn to send his story, she said, "I wish you wouldn't speak so freely about finding me in South Fork. It makes me sound like some sort of object."

"Treasure," David answered promptly, and he reached out his hand to touch her red curls.

She pulled her head away before he could touch her, but not before he said, "Pretty. She was right about that. And you got a position for your mother."

"Yes, I did," Jennie answered. She thought it best not to say more. David was responsible for getting her this position, and it was important for her to keep it. Not only was the work useful, it was also helping her mother and brother survive a very difficult situation. Of course, if Miss Barton really did ask her mother to run the boardinghouses, they would be able to live much better than they were living now.

She begged for an hour at noon to go to her mother to tell her about Miss Barton's visit. Though the reporters were clearly unhappy about letting her go for such a long time, they agreed. As she left the room, they were quarreling about how to deduct the time from their alloted shares. Jennie smiled to think she was so important. There were some things about being a working woman that were actually fun.

Though she slept in the tent with her mother and Peter, it didn't seem like home to Jennie. She was only there for a few hours each night and never saw it in the daytime. Now she looked at it with some attention as she called out to her mother.

Their tent was an eight-by-ten-foot canvas structure supported by wooden poles. She knew that her mother and brother were fairly comfortable there, but whenever the future was mentioned, her mother looked thoughtful. If they had to stay there all winter, it would be terrible, because canvas wouldn't keep out the cold.

Jennie was afraid her mother was worrying too much, while she herself had hardly any time at all to think of the future. All she knew was work from sunrise until midnight, but the reporters were quite generous about money. She was supposed to be earning five dollars a week, and they were giving her all her food plus an extra two dollars a week for her long hours.

Her mother was spending one dollar a week and putting the other six dollars in a tin can buried beneath her pillow. Jennie knew that her wages were keeping them from the kind of despair that other families were facing. Nevertheless it was hard to think of starting all over after working five long years to save $163.

Some folks were saying that the bank would eventually pay back all the money that was lost in the flood. Jennie wasn't sure how they could do that if the records and the currency were buried in the mud. Still, there might be a way.

Ever since the flood it seemed like people were nicer and more honest than they'd been before. Folks who hadn't been very friendly during the last few years were now the fastest of friends. Jennie knew that her mother and Jim Hurst's mother had tea together every day up here on the hillside.

Mrs. Hurst and Jennie's mother were in the same boat these days. The Hursts had also lost their house and all their savings to the deluge of mud that wiped out Johnstown. Now the only real difference between the Hursts and the Brooks was that the Hursts had two grown men who could work to make a new start for their family.

The two mothers were both helping with the children who were left on the hillside while their parents went down into Johnstown to help with the rescue work. It was very useful work to take care of those youngsters, but no one ever thought to offer either woman money, even though there were funds donated to pay rescue operators now.

But to give due credit, not all of the rescue workers were accepting wages. Only those who needed the money to keep body and soul together were taking cash for the digging of mud, dragging of debris, and burying of bodies that occupied most of Johnstown's able-bodied.

All in all, it seemed to Jennie that the people in

Johnstown were more helpful, kinder, more considerate than they had ever been in her sixteen years of life. Class lines melted in the face of the great disaster. Money wasn't of any use to a person if it was buried beneath ten feet of mud.

Mrs. Brooks saw Jennie climbing the hill and began to run toward her. When she got a little closer, Jennie called out, "Nothing is wrong. Don't worry."

Her mother slowed down and put her hand over her heart. She said, "I was afraid there was bad news."

"Nothing like that." Jennie knew her mother was thinking of her aunts. "It's about work. I met Miss Clara Barton, of the Red Cross, and she wants to start some boardinghouses. I told her you were experienced, and she's expecting you to see her today."

Her mother's face broke into a smile so broad that Jennie wanted to cry with joy. It was the first real smile she'd seen on her mother's face in a long time.

"I've got to get back," Jennie said. "They're waiting for me at the brickyard. But I got leave to come and tell you."

Her mother hugged Jennie close and kissed her cheek. She whispered, "Jennie, I am so proud of you."

Jennie's feet were light as she half-ran, half-walked down the hill to the brickyard. She couldn't remember a time when her mother had been so lavish in her praise, and it was a good feeling.

As she re-entered the brickyard she reflected that there were a lot of good things that had come out óf the flood. Jennie was pleased to be earning money, and she felt very grown-up and independent. She didn't want her mother to know how rough and coarse the reporters were, but the truth was that she liked most of them.

One of her favorite reporters was an older man named William Randolph, who smoked thin cigars, and always smelled of whiskey. He seemed a little too old and too literary for the kind of life he was leading.

That afternoon David told her that William Randolph had once been the star reporter for the *New York Times*. "He let the job slip away from him when he got married and settled down," David concluded.

"Do you really think that marriage caused his troubles?" Jennie asked. "Don't you think that drinking spirits had something to do with it?"

David shook his head. "Lots of reporters drink, but not many manage to be settled-down, married men."

"So all good reporters are single gentlemen?" Jennie teased.

"Not all," David's eyes were shining as he teased her back. "Ever hear of a young woman named Nellie Bly?"

"No," Jennie admitted.

"You will," David promised. "Nellie Bly is a brave young woman who will soon be the most famous reporter in the United States. She spent a month in an insane asylum. She pretended to be insane, you know, and she published a series of articles on her experiences. Jolly good idea. I wish I'd thought of it."

Jennie shuddered. "I think it would be awful."

"Of course it's awful," David said. "That's the point. That's what readers want. Look at the Johnstown story. Biggest story since Lincoln was shot. Readers can't get enough of it."

"I think too much is being written about Johnstown," Jennie said. "And I can't imagine why the reporters keep coming."

They now had almost twenty reporters using the brickyard as their headquarters, and the three telegraph operators were still working almost around the clock.

"I've got an idea," David said. "Why don't you give up the boomer trade and take up reporting? You could travel around the world."

Jennie laughed and shook her head. "My poor mother has had a hard enough time adjusting to the fact that I am a telegraph operator. I don't think she would ever adjust to me being a reporter."

"We could be partners," David said.

Jennie flushed at his suggestion and was trying to decide whether it would be better to ignore his improper remark or say something cutting in return.

She liked David and the other reporters, but it was a real problem knowing how to behave around them sometimes. No gentleman would ever make a lady a suggestion such as the one David had just made. But Jennie understood that reporters, even those with good manners like David, weren't exactly gentlemen. The point was that she *was* a lady and expected to be treated like one. What could she say? Suddenly there was a great commotion at the entrance to the building. Jennie was able to turn away from David without showing how upset she was by his silly suggestion.

Chapter Twenty

ONE of the reporters ran in, saying he had a story about a crime that had been committed. Jennie took her place at her desk and began tapping out the story the reporter was dictating excitedly.

According to his story, some men had been caught cutting the fingers off a dead body. He went on to say he had seen a man pulling diamond rings off the body of a woman. According to the story, three diamond rings had been stolen from the body. The reporter rambled as he told his story and eventually said that some "good Johnstown people" charged at the robbers and chased them into the river, where they drowned.

Even as Jennie was typing the story she didn't believe a word of it. Lately she'd begun to suspect that several of the reporters were hanging around the bars that had survived the flood and making up their own stories when they couldn't pick up any easy gossip.

As was her custom, Jennie kept her opinions to herself and tapped out the reporter's story. Then he told her to add that the robbers were Hunkies.

"What do you mean, Hunkies?" Jennie asked.

"You know, Hungarians," the reporter said.

"That can't be true!" Jennie could not help but protest.

"Why not?" the reporter asked.

"Because there are only a few Hungarian families in this town, and they are all very nice people," Jennie protested.

"Are you calling me a liar?" the reporter growled.

"No, no, of course not," Jennie would have liked to say yes but she backed off quickly. She couldn't afford to lose her job, and so she went ahead and typed the story.

Sending out that story made Jennie sick, because she was certain there wasn't a bit of truth in it. There was enough fear and resentment in the world without making up evil stories about people just because they were foreigners.

The next morning when she came to work, the first two stories she sent had to do with thirteen Hungarians who cut off the fingers of a dead and mangled body. In the first story, two of the thirteen were driven to their death by the "angry patriots of Johnstown." In the second story, a total of five foreigners were chased into the surging river.

Later that morning, Jennie compared notes with one of the other telegraph operators and found that he had sent out stories about two blacks being shot by Pittsburgh police as they attempted to loot the dead.

About two o'clock that afternoon, another reporter gave Jennie a similar story, only this time the marauding thieves were Polish. In desperation, Jennie appealed to David, "Can't you stop this foolishness?"

"Reporters have a right to report their views," David said.

"I don't think it's fair to blame Hungarians and other ethnic groups for things like this. There's no proof. As far as I know, there aren't any Polish people or blacks in Johnstown. We do have some Hungarian families in this town, but they have been here quite a while."

"There is a lot of anti-immigrant feeling in the big cities where these fellows are writing their papers," David explained.

"Well, just because the feeling is there doesn't mean that they should add to it," Jennie protested.

"Well, you know you've got to give the readers what they want to read," David said.

"David Winters, are you suggesting that reporters have the right to make up stories, simply because people want to read bad things about certain ethnic groups? There must be something you can do," Jennie pleaded.

"Tell you what, I'll send a story to my paper saying it's all lies. How's that?"

"That's good. But can't you stop them from telling the lies?"

"Sorry." David shook his head.

Jennie did believe that he was sorry, but she also believed that he could do more if he wanted to. She thought it over, holding her temper and trying to figure out what the best thing to do might be. Finally she said, "Well, will you at least tell your reporter friends not to have me send out those stories? They make me sick."

David laughed and nodded in agreement. "I marvel at the way you have the energy to fight, working as hard as you do. You are a very healthy girl. How's that foot?"

Jennie blushed, remembering that it was David who had found her in her petticoat that first day and answered quickly, "My foot is all right now."

"I noticed you are still wearing two different-colored shoes."

This time it was Jennie's turn to laugh, and she said, "I was hoping you wouldn't notice. In fact, I was hoping no one would notice. But one of these days my foot will be healed over and I will be able to wear two matching shoes. And some lucky person will have a pair of good boots when I give these to the salvage pile."

"Best place to take them is up to Clara Barton at the Red Cross," David advised. "She seems to be doing the most systematic work. I had an interview with her earlier this week, but I guess you know all about that."

Jennie laughed. "Yes, I do." David's "interview"

had really been a recap of Miss Barton's visit to the brickyard. He'd written his story as though it had been an exclusive interview. Now Jennie teased him, quoting, " 'She is a small but determined woman.' " Then she added, "Typing your stories, I always know what you've been up to, don't I?"

"Have you thought any more about becoming the second Nellie Bly?" David asked.

Jennie was embarrassed. Instead of answering him, she said, "My mother went to see Clara Barton yesterday. She thinks Miss Barton will let her run the boardinghouses when they are built."

"You didn't answer my question about becoming a reporter," David said. "It's a great life."

Jennie blushed at his suggestion. Didn't he understand how difficult he made it for her when he made jokes like that? If her mother ever dreamed that anyone in the brickyard made such an improper suggestion, she would insist that Jennie quit her position immediately. She decided to answer his question in such a way that he would never ask it again.

"Mr. Winters, you present me with a problem when you ask such personal questions," Jennie said. "I value your friendship, but if you continue to be so presumptuous, you leave me no choice but to discontinue my association with you."

David laughed and held up his hand as though in defense. He said, "I'm sorry. I don't mean to offend you, but there's really nothing unladylike about being a reporter, is there?"

"I will not discuss it." Jennie knew her voice

sounded dignified. She hoped it was cold enough to cut off all discussion without offending David.

David did seem to understand her position, because he didn't bring the subject up again. The two of them chatted for a few more minutes, and then David went out to the street to see what other news he could gather.

For the first time since the flood, there were two telegraph operators idle, and there were no reporters waiting. Jennie decided to take a little time for herself.

She made herself a cup of tea, and she picked up a book that one of the reporters had left on her desk: Walt Whitman's poems. She rather liked Walt Whitman's poems, although he was so modern that her mother preferred not to have her read them. Her mother said he wasn't a suitable writer for a young lady.

Jennie sighed and sipped her tea, thinking about David and his suggestion that she become a reporter. She would never dream of such a thing. Still, she was happy enough breaking conventions to become a telegraph operator. It was hard to know where to draw the line between being modern and being a lady.

It seemed to her that social barriers were much more lax since the flood. Things were very different from what they had been, as was she. Without guilt, she picked up the poems and read for a bit.

That evening was the quietest and easiest that she had spent at the brickyard, and someone actually suggested she might go home at ten o'clock instead of midnight. She took the gift of the extra two hours gratefully and spent the time catching up on her sleep.

The next morning something came in over the wires from New York City that amazed and delighted her. It was a poem by Walt Whitman about the Johnstown flood.

> *A voice from Death, solemn and strange, in*
>   *all his sweep and power*
> *With sudden, indescribable blow—towns*
>   *drown'd — humanity thousands slain,*
> *The vaunted work of thrift, goods, dwellings,*
>   *forge, street, iron bridge,*
> *Dash'd pell-mell by the blow — yet usher'd life*
>   *continuing on . . .*

Tears came to Jennie's eyes as she read the verse, and she was glad to be a part of the work of telegraphing. To be able to read a great poem just written about an event she had lived through seemed truly magical.

That same afternoon, the reporter who had made up the story about the Hungarians came in and filed a long story about Jim Hurst. The way the reporter told the story, Jim was the hero of Johnstown.

The story told how Jim was a local boy who had been sent to college by Robert Matthews and what a fine honor that was. The story then claimed that Jim had been at the South Fork Fishing and Hunting Club on the night the dam had broken. There were direct quotes from Jim about how he had watched the water gush out of the dam hours before the actual disaster.

Then the story went on to say that Jim had single-handedly tried to stop the dam from breaking. When he saw that the break was inevitable, the reporter claimed that Jim had hurried down the hill and run all fourteen miles to Johnstown, shouting, "The dam is breaking! Go to the hills!"

As Jennie tapped out the story she got madder and madder. Worst of all, the reporter claimed that Jim had done his best, and the people of Johnstown had slammed their doors in his face.

Then the story claimed if people had just listened to Jim Hurst, none of the tragedy would have happened. No one would have been killed. Everyone would have been able to head for high ground. The reporter concluded with, "If the ignorant people of Johnstown had listened to the young protégé of their protector, Robert Matthews, this needless tragedy would never have been."

Finally, as the reporter praised Matthews for the wonderful things he had done for Johnstown, Jennie could stand it no more.

She stopped sending her message and said, "Not a word of this is true."

The reporter glared at her and said, "Just type, girly. That's your job."

"Don't call me girly! My name is Miss Brooks!"

"All right, *Miss Brooks*," he said with exaggerated politeness. "Now get this straight. We pay you good money to type the stories, not to criticize them. You are not a reporter, and it is none of your business what we write."

"Yes, sir," she answered but her face was red with fury, and she did not bother to try to hide it.

The reporter was mad enough at Jennie that he began grumbling to other reporters. That day three different reporters warned her to be careful not to anger him. Jennie promised herself that she would not say another word and that she would simply relay whatever messages the reporters chose to write.

She avoided that reporter completely for the next few days, and she didn't try to hide her anger from him. He continued to write stories about the Hungarians, and she told herself she was lucky that she didn't have to send them out. Still, the lies rankled her, and she was increasingly unhappy in her job.

She was angry when other reporters picked up the story about Jim Hurst and embellished on it, calling him the "hero of Johnstown." Though she was grateful to Jim for saving her life, she knew he hadn't been the only hero in the disaster.

She hated the fact that every time anyone used Jim's name, they linked it with Robert Matthews'. It made Jim seem like a puppet. From time to time, she thought of going to see Jim at the morgue, where he was working, but she always backed away from that possibility.

She really didn't have anything to say to Jim, and every time they got together, they quarrelled. Besides, she knew from her mother, who got the news from Jim's mother, that he was working just as hard or harder than she was. This was no time to try to talk, especially about the South Fork Fishing and Hunting Club members' responsibility for the disaster.

She couldn't just go chasing after Jim, anyway. If he wanted to see her, he could find her. She was living very close to where his mother and father were camped. Of course, she had to admit to herself that she was seldom home.

The more the reporters wrote about Jim, the more she thought about him, and that made her angry, too. Why couldn't she just forget him? They had seldom spoken a civil word to each other, and he obviously wasn't seriously interested in her. Jim Hurst was an ambitious man — that was clear enough. He would be interested in one of the daughters of one of his bosses.

Thinking those kinds of thoughts made her furious. She was angry and dismayed at how the reporters seemed to think that the dam breaking was an act of nature.

One evening she asked David, as he walked her home to her tent, "Don't they know that the members of the South Fork Fishing and Hunting Club didn't repair the dam properly? Why don't they report that?"

"Some know that and some don't," David said. "Reporters are just like anyone else, Jennie, they have their own peculiar way of looking at things. Now you say it was the South Fork Fishing and Hunting Club that caused the dam to break, but there are plenty of folks who think that it was foolish for Johnstown people to keep rebuilding on the same ground. They think the citizens of Johnstown are equally to blame.

"It is a matter of public record that they have had lots of floods here, and instead of building on higher ground, they just kept right on building here in the valley. Nobody can deny that that is foolish, can they? But no one is angry at the people of Johnstown."

"I am," Jennie admitted, "I am mad at them all." In her heart she knew that it was true that she had a lot of anger toward the Johnstown people for being so foolish. But she was even more angry with Robert Matthews and his cronies for being so selfish. And she was angry with Jim Hurst for being so certain that his boss was right, in spite of all the evidence to the contrary. She realized that she was angry with just about everyone, including the reporters who didn't tell the truth.

She laughed at herself and said aloud, "I guess the only one that I'm not mad at is Clara Barton. As far as I can see, everything she has done has been all right."

David agreed and said, "Yes, she has certainly put the American Red Cross on the map with this, hasn't she?"

The next morning her mother told her that she was planning to go to work for Clara Barton in two days. "I can take Peter with me, and there is so much to be done. I'll be in charge of one of the outdoor kitchens until the boardinghouses are finished."

"Oh, Mother, are you sure you're strong enough?" Jennie didn't want to admit it, but her mother had looked frail ever since the night of the flood. And she had a persistent cough that worried Jennie a great deal.

"Yes, I'm sure, my dear. I think it would be good for me to do something useful."

"But you're very useful here."

"Let Mrs. Hurst and some of the other women who don't need to earn money watch the children," her mother said. "I can't have you bear the burden alone."

"I don't mind," Jennie said. "In fact, I like working."

Her mother frowned and shook her head, "That is what I fear the most, my dear. I certainly wouldn't want you to choose a life like your poor, dear aunt Hester's."

"You've worked all your life, Mother. I'd like to be in a position to take care of you."

Her mother smiled and said, "Don't you worry about me, Jennie, I've been having something of a picnic the last few days. I've been lying in bed and playing with the children, and I'm quite well rested now."

Privately Jennie doubted that anyone could have much of a picnic in the midst of the confusion, the smells, the disaster that was constantly all around them. She hated to think of her mother leaving the clear air of the hillside and going down into the dank city, but she thought that her mother was probably as healthy as many of the other people who were working with Clara Barton. Besides, her mother was as strong-minded in her own way as Jennie was, so Jennie did not protest further.

When Jennie went to work the next morning, there were two more telegraph operators in the brickyard. One was sitting at her desk, and for one horrible moment she was afraid she had been dismissed.

It was quickly apparent that the reporters expected her to be pleased by the new operators. William Randolph said, "Now you can have a day off, Missy. What will you do with it?"

Jennie was stunned at the idea of having a whole day off. It would be the first one since the night of the flood, and she thought of a million things that she could or should do. She laughed and said, "I guess I'll sleep. That will be the best, won't it?"

"Not today," David laughed. "You have to break in the new boomers today, but you can have to-morrow off. Sleep all day if you want."

She did sleep until eleven o'clock on the morning of her precious day off, and then she got up and washed her hair before she took a walk. Instead of walking toward Johnstown and all of the memories of disaster, she walked up into the hills, to the village of Bright Creek, where she had heard her friend Millie was staying.

Jennie had not seen Millie since the flood, though she had heard news of her. She was living with her grandmother's cousin because every member of her family was lost. When the two girls greeted each other, they hugged as though they were dear sisters.

They sat on the front porch of Millie's new home and told each other of their adventures. Like most people in the Johnstown area, most of the conversation was about where they had been in the flood. For the first time, Jennie related her whole adventurous trip down the flooded gorge.

Millie sat in rapt attention until Jennie's story was over. Then she asked, "And will you marry David Winters or Jim Hurst?"

"Neither." Jennie laughed at the idea.

"But you have two suitors to choose from. How lucky you are, Jennie."

She shook her head and said, "Neither is a suitor. David is much too involved in his work. For that matter, so is Jim. And I could never marry a man like David Winters — he is much too lighthearted."

"But Jim? He is not lighthearted?"

Again Jennie laughed and shook her head. "I can't even talk with Jim Hurst for ten minutes without quarrelling with him. The idea of marrying him is preposterous. Besides, this is no time to think of marriage."

Millie's eyes suddenly filled with tears. "It is all I *can* think of. My cousin is kind, but she clearly doesn't want me. Every plan I've ever had is destroyed now. There is no money for schooling so I can't be a schoolteacher. I fear I must marry quickly."

"But surely you can stay here!"

"Not for long, I fear. My parents were never close to my cousin, and now that they are gone, there is only duty to bind us. Duty does not sit well." The tears fell freely now as Millie talked.

Jennie took her hand. She would have liked to offer her friend a home, but truthfully she had none to offer. Miss Clara Barton would certainly not welcome an extra person. The girls sat quietly, letting Millie's tears fall into the soft green grass of the Pennsylvania summer.

Millie spoke softly, "I think that my cousin wishes me gone already but does not know how to tell me. I don't know what I shall do."

"Something will turn up," Jennie said. "You will find work."

"There is nothing for me here, nothing at all."

Jennie recognized the truth of Millie's words. The only jobs in town for women were in teaching, and there were many more educated women than there were teaching jobs. The only other job was running a boardinghouse, and for that you needed to be a respectable widow, not a sixteen-year-old girl. No one in Johnstown would hire a servant like Millie because they would be uncomfortable having a girl of their own class working for them in that way.

Millie said, "I've racked my brain, asking myself what I should do, and I am about ready to send away to see if I can find a husband."

"Oh!" Jennie cried, "you wouldn't!"

"Yes, I have the newspaper right here," Millie said. "This gentleman seems like a nice man." She ran into the house, and she brought back the *Phil-*

adelphia Gazette, and on the back page there was a long list of confidential ads, one of which read: *Respectable widower with two small children seeks healthy young wife for Christian home.*

"I've written to him," Millie admitted, "and I have told him about my situation."

Jennie was appalled that Millie would feel desperate enough to do a thing like that. But she had absolutely no other suggestions to offer her. Finally she said, "Maybe I could teach you telegraphing."

Millie shook her head, "They don't really want women. I heard that Pittsburgh found out the operator in Merryman was a woman, and they dismissed her."

Jennie sighed. She had heard exactly the same rumor last week, so it was probably true. As far as she knew, she was the only female telegraph operator in Pennsylvania, now that her aunt Hester was gone.

It was growing dark, and the friends parted without solving Millie's problem. As Jennie walked down the path toward her hillside encampment, she thanked her lucky stars that she had family left. She was glad that she wasn't faced with the possibility of being totally alone in the world.

The idea of marrying someone you didn't know seemed horrible to Jennie, and yet it might very well be the best solution available to Millie. A girl's life in the big city was a hard one, and there just weren't very many things that she could do to earn a living that was respectable.

Jennie thought that the reporters she worked for

were doing a pretty good job of covering the Johnstown flood when it came to the ordinary people, except that they always seemed to go after the wild extremes. Why didn't anyone ever tell the simple stories like Millie's?

The next day at work, she told David, "You know, no one has written about how ordinary people's lives are affected. I have a friend who's thinking of marrying a stranger because her family were all killed, and she has no place to go. My mother was fairly comfortable running a boardinghouse, and now she's working like a servant for the Red Cross. The flood even changed the lives of comfortable housewives like Mrs. Hurst, who used to have a servant of her own and now takes care of other people's children. I think you should do a series on women's lives and show the changes."

David looked at her quizically and cocked his head to one side. He said, "That's a good idea. Could I talk to your friend?"

"Oh, no, no, no," Jennie said. "She would die of embarrassment. Go out and find your own people to interview."

"Well, that is something of a problem with respectable young ladies, isn't it?" David teased. "They're not terribly brave about telling much about their personal lives. Why don't I start with you? How has your personal life changed since the flood?"

Jennie laughed and said, "I have no personal life."

"What about that young man who was visiting you the first time I met you?"

"Jim? He's not even a friend, really."

"Not a friend?" David raised an eyebrow quizzically. "It seems to me that he would like to be your friend."

"Maybe he would," Jennie answered, "but I cannot be friends with anyone who is such a toady to big business."

David threw back his head and roared with laughter and said, "Your views are quite radical for such a nice young lady. Did you form them on your own?"

"I formed my views by observation of the factory owners," Jennie said. "You know this isn't the first flood Johnstown has had. My father was killed in a flood five years ago. That's why my mother runs a boardinghouse — or *ran* a boardinghouse."

"Your father was killed in a flood?" David said.

"Yes, he was trying to save some machinery that belonged to the company. The flood came very quickly, and he was caught under a piece of machinery and killed."

"When was that?"

"It was on a Saturday in July, five years ago, 1884. After my father's death my whole world changed. My mother had to go to work and I had to work before and after school. Then I dropped out of school when I was twelve years old. I've been working with my mother in the boardinghouse ever since. It has been a very difficult time, and now this flood will make it even worse."

"Ah, but now you're a boomer. You have a different occupation, my dear."

"I've asked you not to call me that." Jennie wished

that David could carry on a serious conversation without turning it to something light. It amazed her how a man as handsome and elegant and intelligent as he could take such a casual attitude toward life.

"All right, you're not a boomer, you're a telegraph operator and you can make a good living doing that."

"When the flood is over and all you reporters leave town there will be a lot more telegraph operators than there will be jobs, I'm afraid."

"Well, maybe the telegraph office will give you your aunt Hester's job," David pointed out. "You and your mother could move to South Fork."

Jennie shuddered at the idea of going to work in the South Fork telegraph office. She knew that it would be an opportunity, but it was lonely work. More than that, Jennie knew that the memory of the flood would always be with her if she were to do that.

"I won't worry about that today," Jennie said, "I'll just worry about getting the stories onto the wires."

"Good," David said. "I've got a great one about a young woman named Mary who has to put an ad in the paper for a husband because she has no place to live. We'll call it the 'Tearful Romance'."

"You wouldn't!" Jennie laughed.

"I would if I weren't afraid you'd never speak to me again," David admitted. "It's a great yarn."

Chapter
Twenty-one

JENNIE saw Jim Hurst when she was walking down the street with David Winters. Jim came toward them from the other direction. He looked so tired that she barely recognized him. He carried a sack over his shoulder, and he looked as stooped as an old man. When he drew closer he put his sack down on the path and called out, "Jennie!"

Jennie stopped and put out her hand and said, "Hello, Jim. You remember David?"

David laughed and said, "Why, I guess neither one of us is ever going to forget our adventure, are we?"

Jim nodded in agreement and wiped sweat off his brow.

Jennie could not help but compare the handsome

elegance of David with Jim's rugged looks. She supposed it was unfair to think it, but David was a young man who would turn anyone's head. Jim looked tired and ordinary.

The two young men seemed to be looking at each other as though they were deciding whether to be friends or rivals. Jennie was amused at their obvious competition.

She said, "David wrote a newspaper story that I sent out to the newspapers about your adventure at the railroad. I understand you helped him clear the train."

Jim raised one eyebrow and smiled slightly. David looked embarrassed and said, "I might have colored that one a bit, but you are the hero of several other stories. I suppose you know you made the front page of the *New York Times*?"

"No." Jim didn't seem very interested.

Jennie said, "You are the hero of Johnstown, according to a lot of the reporters. Haven't you seen any of those stories they've been sending out about you?"

Jim shook his head and said, "I've been working very hard."

David said, "I suppose I might have written more about you myself, I'm sorry about that. But Jennie has such firm ideas about the South Fork Hunting and Fishing Club members being the ones at fault that I've been influenced by her, I suppose."

Jim looked bewildered and tired.

Jennie explained to him, trying to keep the bitterness out of her voice. "You're famous, Jim. You got written up in the Pittsburgh papers as the protégé of Robert Matthews. The story said you tried to save the people of Johnstown, that it was their own foolishness which killed them."

"I don't have time to read the newspapers," Jim said.

Jennie wondered what he and the other citizens of Johnstown would make of the hundreds of thousands of words pouring out of Johnstown to the rest of the world. People in Johnstown were much too busy to read the stories. Most of them weren't aware of the debate that was raging in the press right now about who was responsible for the dam bursting.

For a while it had been impossible to establish who the members of the South Fork Hunting and Fishing Club even were. The known members had made a real effort not to talk to reporters at all.

Most of the members who did talk to reporters spent all their time denying that the club had any responsibility for the tragedy. Some of the more foolish ones had even claimed that the dam didn't really burst at all.

Conflict about who was to blame was a major portion of the stories being filed in the papers right now. One reporter had filed a story proclaiming that the flood had nothing at all to do with the dam breaking. And now a different reporter had brought in a copy of a newspaper which proclaimed in bold headlines, *CLUB GUILTY*.

One lawsuit had already been filed by a Johnstown widow against the club members. Several other citizens of Johnstown were threatening to sue, even though most people agreed that no court in Pittsburgh would ever find the influential club members guilty of negligence. Many people honestly believed they weren't guilty at all.

Jennie knew that most of the reporters preferred to believe that the dam failure was an act of nature and not the fault of the club. She had long ago figured out that their opinions were based on several factors, including how close to Pittsburgh their papers were. Not one Pittsburgh reporter had written anything bad about the South Fork Fishing and Hunting Club.

David, who wrote for a Philadelphia paper, had been the most outspoken reporter except for those who wrote for the *New York Times* and other out-of-state papers.

Jennie would have liked to tell Jim some of these things, except he looked so tired she took pity on him. She knew what Jim thought, so there seemed no real reason to talk about it. And no matter what he had done in the past, he was certainly doing his best to make amends these days. She knew from her mother that he hardly stopped long enough to sleep, he was so busy with rescue work.

David said, "But now that we've run into each other, I'd like to interview you. Shouldn't pass up a chance to talk to the 'Hero of Johnstown', should I?"

Jim shook his head in dismay and picked up the gunnysack he'd been carrying. He said, "I can't worry about that. I'm supervising the clearing of the debris down by the stone bridge."

Whenever the people of Johnstown mentioned the stone bridge, they dropped their voice in horror. The collection of debris was still piled high in front of the bridge where Jennie had almost lost her life.

The authorities had insisted that the best thing to do was let the fire burn as long as possible, thereby eliminating health hazards. For days the flames reminded the Johnstown survivors of the screams of their trapped loved ones.

The fire had burned itself out by now, and the screams had long ago stopped, but they were implanted forever in the minds of the Johnstown survivors.

"I say, old man," David asked, "is that dynamite in that gunnysack?"

"Yes," Jim answered. "We've been trying to dislodge the debris piece by piece," Jim explained. "Not with much success, I must add. We have a dynamite expert coming this afternoon. I'm to help him."

Jennie was surprised at the sharp fear that ran through her at the thought of Jim working with dynamite.

David frowned and said, "Be careful, dynamite can be dangerous."

"I'll be fine," Jim answered.

"Jim, you look tired," Jennie said. "Are you getting enough sleep? And you look thin. Are you getting enough to eat?"

Jim's eyes caught hers, and there was gratitude and love shining through them as he answered, "The construction crews are fed well."

"You're working with a construction crew?" David asked. "I thought you were Matthews' right-hand man."

Jim ignored the reporter and asked Jennie, "Are you enjoying your work in the telegraph office?"

"I'll say she is," David answered for her. "She's the best boomer we've ever had. All the men are crazy about her."

David's voice was proprietary, and Jennie flushed, hoping that Jim wouldn't assume David had a right to speak for her. She had grown somewhat used to David's brash ways, but there was no reason to think that Jim would understand.

She spoke directly to Jim, ignoring David entirely, "I'm very fortunate to have a job. The hours are long, but the work pays well. I try to count my blessings."

"Yes, I guess we're all counting our blessings these days," Jim said shortly. Then he looked from Jennie to David and back again.

There was a long, uncomfortable silence, and then Jim said, "Give my regards to your mother." They walked on in opposite directions.

Later that afternoon, the dynamiting began in earnest, and during the next five days there were intermittent blasts that upset the whole community.

Every time one of the booms went off, Jennie thought of Jim and how tired he looked. It was hard for her to think of him looking so much older than his nineteen years.

More than one story was filed about the dynamiting that week. Some of the stories claimed that the dynamiting was causing more damage than it was helping. There were stories about Arthur Kirk, the expert who had come to Johnstown to supervise the clearing work.

Kirk was soon dubbed "The Prince of Dynamiters," by the reporters, and he was quoted often. Some of the stories spoke of pieces of bodies flying through the air as the dynamite dislodged the debris. Other stories talked about the strange cry that Kirk emitted just before he set off a blast.

Jennie tapped out the stories, trying to ignore the dangers to the dynamiters that they recounted. However she was relieved when she passed on a story five days later that said that Kirk and his crew had been dismissed and were to be replaced by Major Phillips.

Citizens of Johnstown hated the dynamiting and began to call for the arrest of Phillips and his band of workers, because they were blasting at night as well as in the daytime. The furor over the dynamiting filled the reporters' needs for more and more interesting stories to send to their newspapers.

By the end of June a channel was cleared, and the water could run under the bridge. Major Phillips began to use coal oil instead of dynamite to clear the rest of the debris, and the townspeople slept better.

By the first of July, there was an official estimate

of the dead, which came to over two thousand people. There was a long list of unidentified bodies and an even longer list of persons who were missing, but it now seemed impossible that the two lists would ever be matched together.

Jennie could see from the stories that went through her telegraph office that things were more or less returning to normal. Many of the stories were about the magnificent donations that came from all over the world. Some of them were small, like the $101 that came from the town of Tombstone, Arizona. Others were very large, like the $20,000 that came from the New York Stock Exchange.

She heard from her mother that Jim was hoping to be relieved from his position with the dynamiters very soon, and she was glad that the danger was over. She found that she worried about him a lot, and though she tried to tell herself it was only because he'd saved her life, she knew she'd breathe easier when he was off that dangerous duty.

Chapter
Twenty-two

One evening Jennie and her mother had a long talk about Aunt Hester and Aunt Nettie. Her mother began it by saying, "I just can't believe they won't walk in that door one day."

"We haven't heard one of those stories in weeks," Jennie said quietly. "The miraculous reappearances seemed to have stopped."

"But they never found any sign of them."

"The relief squads didn't find any sign of almost a thousand people," Jennie reminded her mother.

The next Sunday morning, she and her mother and brother held a private service for their aunts.

They walked to her father's gravesite and said some simple prayers. Then they joined hands and sang some hymns.

After their service, they went to church as a family for the first time since the flood. The church was almost empty, but it felt good to Jennie to be back in their familiar routine.

She noticed several strangers among the congregation, and she supposed they were a part of the thousands of workmen, soldiers, morticians, and medical personnel who had been brought to Johnstown to clear up the damage.

When they came out of church that Sunday, Jim was waiting on the steps. He walked directly over to them and said, "My mother told me you were coming to church today. I'm sorry I didn't wake up in time to attend the service."

"You look rested," Jennie said. She was glad to see that Jim had recovered most of his youthful good looks. He had lost that exhausted look.

"Will you take a walk with me, Jennie?" Jim asked. Before she could reply, he turned to her mother and said, "I'd like to take your daughter for a walk, if I have your permission."

Mrs. Brooks nodded her head. She was obviously pleased by Jim's good manners.

"I have things to do at home," Jennie protested. Actually, she had very little to do. There were enough telegraph operators now so that she was working only twelve hours a day. She had clean clothes and polished boots.

"Come walk with me," Jim said. Then he looked

down at her feet and asked, "Can you walk a distance? Is your foot healed?"

"Her foot's been healed for weeks," Mrs. Brooks said. "Now you young people go and have a good time."

There was no real way that Jennie could refuse the invitation, since her mother insisted that she go. As she nodded her head in acceptance, it occurred to her that her mother and Jim's mother had probably planned this whole encounter. The two of them were quite good friends since the flood. The Hursts had found a way to rent a house in town again, and Mrs. Hurst dropped in to have tea with Jennie's mother almost daily.

Jennie was afraid to say anything to Jim because she didn't want to quarrel, so she walked silently. Jim may have had the same fears, because he was also quiet as they turned from the church and walked out of town and up the road toward the hill towns.

They passed several makeshift refugee camps before they were high enough up to find a quiet place. Finally they stopped at the crest of a hill and looked down onto the valley below.

They stood and looked down into the town. Even from that distance, the town looked topsy-turvy. Jennie said, "It looks as though a giant came in one night and picked up buildings and put them in the wrong places."

"Yes," Jim agreed with her and said nothing else. Suddenly, he sighed and added, "It is a beautiful valley."

"It *was*," Jennie corrected.

"It will be again," Jim said. "The relief workers are doing a fine job. And money has come from so many sources."

"Over three million dollars," Jennie said. "A reporter totalled it up the other day."

"The restoration work will be done before the winter," Jim said. "The important thing is to get everyone inside before the snows come."

The two young people spent some time pointing out familiar and unfamiliar sites to each other. The river was still swollen, but the waters had receded enough to make most of the main streets of Johnstown look like mud flats.

Among other buried and displaced buildings, Jim pointed out the Johnstown Bank. He said, "I hear they've started returning money to people. Eventually everyone will be repaid."

"That's wonderful news," Jennie said. It seemed funny to her that she had her fingertips on every story that was going out to the world, but she didn't know the news that meant the most to her and her family. She laughed softly.

"What's funny?" Jim asked.

"Nothing much," Jennie said. "But it's a beautiful day, and I am glad to be alive. Look, over there. The bridge is almost clear now."

The debris was still shoved up against the dam, but the river ran swiftly through the openings. They could see men running to and fro, working to clear even more of the debris away. "What a lot of workers there are," Jennie exclaimed.

"Yes," Jim said. "They don't need me anymore."

"You know, I can hardly believe this has really happened," Jennie confided. "The town is down there looking like someone crumpled it into a new shape, and I've been sending stories out for six weeks, and I still don't quite believe it all."

Jim agreed, "It will take years before we really understand what happened. Everything here has changed so much. When I come back, it will be to a totally different town."

"Are you going somewhere?" Jennie asked. Why was her mouth dry when she asked the question?

"Yes. I've been offered a scholarship to an engineering school in New York. It will be very advanced work for me."

"You're leaving?" Jennie was so startled she could hardly take in the news.

"Yes," Jim said, "there's nothing special that I need to do here. There are plenty of men to take my place, and I've been offered a full scholarship."

"Where did the scholarship come from?" she asked.

"Robert Matthews," Jim admitted. "I received a letter from his assistant last week."

"You're going to take it?" Jennie asked. She was horrified.

"Yes."

"Don't you know that anything that comes from those people has the blood of Johnstown on it?"

"Jennie, this is an opportunity I can't miss," Jim said. "It's the best engineering school in the nation."

"I don't care if it is the best engineering school

in the world," Jennie answered. "I can't imagine why you would accept anything from a man like Robert Matthews."

"Jennie, he's just a man like any other man," Jim argued. "You make Matthews sound like a devil."

"He is a devil," Jennie snapped. "I thought after the dam broke you would break your association with him."

"I did plan to resign, but it's not fair to blame one man for the negligence of a whole group of people. Even if the members of the South Fork Fishing and Hunting Club are held liable, Matthews is just one member."

"They will surely be counted liable," Jennie said. "But even if the legal courts absolve them, they are guilty."

"Jennie, let's be friends," Jim pleaded. He held out his hands to her and added, "I'm leaving Johnstown tomorrow, and I care too much for you to say good-bye in anger."

She put her hands behind her back. He reached up and touched a lock of her red hair. For one moment Jennie thought he was going to kiss her.

She drew back in alarm and said, "Jim Hurst, I don't know what I have to say to you to make you understand. I don't approve of the choices you've made."

"You're the only person I really care about saying good-bye to," he said. He put his hand on the back of her neck and drew her closer to him.

As he bent down to kiss her, she pulled away and

almost shouted, "I don't want to be the only person you want to say good-bye to."

"Is it because of that reporter?" Jim asked.

"No, it isn't!" Jennie answered loudly. "That reporter, whose name you know very well, will also be leaving town soon. David means nothing to me."

"And I mean nothing to you, either?"

"Nothing." Jennie stared at Jim, thinking of a thousand other things she could say. Then the hurt look on his face made her reconsider. Life was cruel enough without adding to anyone's pain. The flood had taught her that much.

She paused and gave herself time to think honestly. Then she said quietly, "Jim, you must mean something to me, because I think about you often. We've been friends for a long time, and I get so angry with you that I think you must mean something to me."

Jim smiled broadly, and he looked so happy that Jennie wanted to make sure he understood what she was saying. "But I don't want to encourage a friendship when we have such different ideas about things. I wouldn't want to encourage you to believe. . . ."

He broke off her words by putting his fingertips on her lips and smiling as he tilted her chin upwards. He looked down at her, and she could see the love in his eyes. He had such deep blue eyes, and they seemed so true that she almost felt herself melt into his arms.

The love from his eyes warmed her. How easy it

would be simply to agree with him, and from this time forward she could let him make all of the decisions. How good it would be to let someone else take care of her, to have a strong man in charge of her life.

He bent to kiss her again, and she drew back abruptly, as though she had suddenly leaned too far over the edge of a cliff. She said, "I must go back now."

She turned and began to run down the hill. Jim soon caught up with her and grabbed her around the waist. She struggled and then he let her go. He laughed as he said, "I won't steal a kiss you refuse to give freely."

She tried to frown but his laughter made her feel young and happy. Her frown turned into a half-smile.

"I want to write to you, Jennie," Jim said. "Will you read my letters?"

Jennie felt a struggle deep within herself. As she tried to read the conflict within her own heart, she could feel how deeply Jim cared for her. It surprised and impressed her that he could be so certain of his feelings. If she said yes, he would write. She knew he would continue to pursue her until she promised to marry him.

Finally, she said, "I'd rather you didn't write, Jim."

"But will you read my letters if I do write?" he persisted. "I have no one else to write to."

"You have your mother," she answered.

"I have no friend my own age," Jim corrected

himself. "There were few left, and many were killed in the flood. Those that survived have moved on to California or other places."

Jennie knew that was not quite true. She smiled at Jim's persistence. It was flattering to have someone pursue her this way.

"Will you read my letters?" Jim asked. "You can send me the news."

Jennie was silent while she tested her true feelings. They had been through so much together. And she owed him her life. How could she refuse such a simple request? Finally she said, "Yes, I'll read your letters, Jim, but I won't promise to write back."

"Your promise to read them is enough," Jim said. He took her hands in his, pulled her close to him, and very gently kissed her on the forehead, then kissed one cheek, and then the other.

Jennie held very still while he kissed her. His lips felt soft and warm and sweet on her face. When he kissed her lips, she lifted her face toward his eagerly, and then she remembered herself and pulled away.

Jennie ran almost all the way down the hill with Jim in pursuit. When he caught up with her, her face was flushed. She was surprised that she had let him take such liberties, and she knew that her mother would be horrified.

Jim caught her hand, and Jennie glared at him. "Let go of me! You had no right to kiss me!" she said.

Jim laughed. "I had no right, but it wasn't really wrong either, you know."

"You're no gentleman, Jim Hurst."

He laughed again and said, "Yes, I am. Would you like me to propose marriage right now to prove it?"

"Of course not! I'd never marry you!"

"Yes, you will," Jim promised. "But I won't insist you make up your mind today. It's enough that you've promised to write to me."

"I promised to read your letters, not write!" Jennie couldn't tell whether she was really angry or just pretending to be to cover her embarrassment about the kiss.

"Don't be mad, Jennie. Come on, I'll walk you back to your new boardinghouse."

"I'd rather walk alone," Jennie answered.

Jim caught her hand again and asked, "Will you kiss me good-bye, Jennie?"

"Of course not," she said. But Jim had already gathered her in his arms. She was honest enough to admit she liked the feel of his arms around her and the touch of his lips on hers. For one brief moment, she returned his kiss, and then she pulled away. Picking up her skirts, she ran the rest of the way home alone.

Chapter
Twenty-three

J ENNIE tried not to think about Jim during the next weeks. She hadn't seen very much of him before he left, so it was easy to pretend he was still in Johnstown. It was when she thought of him as being far away that she realized how lonely she felt.

Ten days after he left, Jennie received her first letter, and it gave her a very strange feeling to turn it over in her hand and look at the postmark from New York City. She opened the letter immediately.

Most of the letter was about his travels to New York and how the people he met were all so curious about what had happened to him in Johnstown. She smiled as she read how people treated him like a hero.

He asked her to give his regards to her "reporter

friends" and thank them for their "exaggerated stories" about his exploits. He concluded the letter by saying that he was now sure that the scholarship he'd accepted was an attempt by the members of the South Fork Fishing and Hunting Club to gain favorable recognition, but he intended to make the most of the opportunity.

His letter contained nothing very personal, but he ended it by saying he hoped she was thinking of him. Jennie folded the letter thoughtfully and sat down at her desk to write to him immediately. She had said she wouldn't promise to write, but she had to.

She filled her letter with news about Johnstown and gossip about their few mutual friends who were left in town. She said nothing at all about their ongoing quarrel about the responsibility for the dam breaking. There was really no sense discussing the things they had agreed to disagree about.

She posted her letter to Jim the next morning before she set out to visit her friend Millie. It was her day off, and she was anxious about her friend.

When she got to her destination, she found Millie sitting on the porch, waiting for her. Millie called out, "I saw you climbing the hill. I'm so glad!"

Jennie could see that Millie's eyes were filled with excitement. As soon as she drew close enough, Millie took her hand and said, "I've had a letter from him and he sounds like such a nice man. Would you like to read it?"

Jennie laughed and said yes. The two girls went

into the house, and Millie took a letter out of the kitchen cupboard, where she had hidden it behind the sugar bowl.

As they went back to the porch Millie said, "Since I have no room of my own here, I find the kitchen is the safest place. I do all the cooking and housework, since I've come to live with my cousin."

They giggled like two young schoolgirls as they sat down on the porch, and Millie unfolded the letter. Jennie could tell by the way the creases were worn that the letter was well read.

"His name is Charles Whitmore," Millie said in a reverent voice. She handed the letter to Jennie as though it were a priceless treasure.

The letter said, *My dear Miss Washington, since your recent tragedy in Johnstown has no doubt driven you to write to me, I must answer promptly for fear of losing you. My name is Charles Whitmore and I am thirty-five years old.*

Jennie's heart sank at the idea that Millie would be marrying someone nineteen years older than she was. She forced herself to keep smiling as she read on.

> *My children, Efram, Eliza, and Louise, are seventeen, twelve, and ten years old, respectively. Efram, the oldest, is actually my stepchild. I was his mother's second husband; she was a few years older than I. We had a very happy marriage, and I learned that age is of little or no consequence. I hope that you will*

*feel the same, as you are a very young woman.
My farm is in the southeastern section of
Iowa, and I grow corn and grain. When the
weather is good the crops are bountiful. Re-
cently I bought a thresher, and I have four
hired men working for me. Would you send a
photograph in your next letter? Sincerely,
Charles Whitmore.*

"He sent his photograph," Millie said. She handed
Jennie a small brown photograph of a dark-
eyed man with a heavy mustache and heavy eye-
brows.

Jennie thought he looked kind, but he did look
old enough to be Millie's father. It broke her heart
to think that Millie was marrying a man whose step-
son was one year older than she was.

Jennie said, "He looks very nice."

Millie hugged her and said, "Oh, Jennie, I think
he is the answer to a young girl's prayer. Don't you
think he has kind eyes?"

Jennie agreed that he had kind eyes. Then they
talked a bit about how to obtain a photograph. Jennie suggested that she come down to the newspaper
office the next day, and that one of the reporters
who could use a camera would take her photograph
for a very small sum.

"But I have no money!" Millie wailed. "None at
all."

"I have some," Jennie offered.

Millie shook her head quickly and said, "I couldn't take your money."

Jennie thought for a moment, and then she said, "Millie, do you have a dress that you would sell me? I have only this one dark green dress. I have been wearing my mother's extra dress sometimes, but between the two of us we have only three dresses. Perhaps you have a dress you would sell me for a dollar."

Millie's eyes lit up at the idea. "I have four dresses." She went to a box that was tucked under the table in the kitchen and pulled out her dresses. The first was a soft blue one that Jennie longed to touch. Millie put it back quickly, saying, "I shall be married in that."

Jennie swallowed her disappointment and waited as Millie looked deeper into the box and pulled out a grey dress with pink ribbons around the neck and around the sleeves. She offered it to Jennie, asking, "Will this do for a dollar?"

"Oh, yes!" Jennie said. It was a pretty dress, and though it was a bit worn it would make a nice change.

"Don't you want to try it on?" Millie offered. But Jennie said she was sure it would be all right since they were the same size.

The girls agreed that Millie should come to the newspaper office the next day, and Jennie would give her a dollar.

The next day when Millie came to the office she was wearing her best blue dress, and she had obviously gone to a lot of trouble to get her hair just right for this occasion. It was in little curls and ringlets all around her head, and she looked quite excited and pretty.

Millie had to stand still for a long time for the photographer. He put her head in a brace to hold it still and told her to hold her breath while he was taking the photograph.

While Millie was holding still, David came by and whispered, "Is that your friend who's getting married?"

"Don't you dare say a word to her," Jennie whispered back. She didn't like the mischievous gleam in David's eye at all.

When Millie's ordeal was over, the photographer said, "Come on, Jennie, I'll take yours, too."

"I have no one to send a photograph to," Jennie protested.

"You can keep it," Millie said.

"I have no money," Jennie said. She was excited and a little frightened by the idea of having her photograph taken.

"It doesn't matter," the photographer said. "A pretty girl like you will have someone to send a photograph to soon enough."

While Jennie stood with her head in the brace, she kept thinking about Jim Hurst and wondering if she would eventually end up sending the photograph to him. Somehow she thought she might.

The two girls took a stroll down the main street of town after having their photos taken. They looked at the progress Miss Clara Barton was making with her rescue work and stopped in to have tea with Jennie's mother. Then Millie went home to pack, because she was leaving in two days.

Jennie went back to work, feeling quite sad about the fact that Millie would be leaving so soon. When she got there, David asked, "Why so sad, Jennie?"

"Everyone's leaving," she said.

David looked pensive for a moment, and then he said, "I'll be leaving very soon myself."

"Oh, David! I will miss you!" Jennie was close to tears.

"Come with me," David said suddenly.

"You know I'd never consider such a thing."

"As my wife," David offered. "Wouldn't you like to be Mrs. David Winters? I'll be a very famous reporter one day."

Jennie laughed.

"I'm serious, you know. I've had two small notes from the *New York Times* this week. I expect they'll be asking me to come to work for them very soon."

"I wouldn't be surprised," Jennie said. She had learned never to take anything David said seriously unless it was about reporting. That was his whole life.

Chapter
Twenty-four

JENNIE saw Millie off at the train station. As she waited for the train, Millie said, "I'm sorry to leave you, but I'll be so glad to get out of Johnstown. I think I will be able to smell this town to the end of my days."

"I don't think so," Jennie said, "I think you'll have a happy new life where you are and forget about this."

"Forget about the death of my mother and father? Forget about the death of my brothers and sisters? Forget about the death and destruction we all lived through?"

"No," Jennie said quickly. "Not the death of your loved ones. But I think that you will go on and have a happy life of your own. That's all I was saying."

Millie nodded her head and said, "Oh, I wish you could come with me to Iowa. Shall I write Mr. Whitmore and see if he has a brother?"

Jennie laughed at the idea and said, "No, I'm too young to marry." She thought of David's joking proposal and Jim's serious intentions and frowned. She wasn't so very young after all. "And I have my mother and my brother here, and I must take care of them. It's different for you, because you are all alone."

"Yes," Millie agreed. Her eyes filled with tears as the train pulled into the station and the porter came over to help her with her one bag. She kissed Jennie good-bye and climbed on the train to go to her new life.

That evening Jennie told her mother all about sending her friend off to get married. Then she showed her mother the two photographs of herself which the photographer had been kind enough to give her. She said, "I don't know what to do with these."

"I would like to have a photograph of you, dear," Mrs. Brooks said.

"You have me," Jennie said.

"For when you are grown-up and gone away."

"Gone away? I'm not going anywhere," Jennie answered with a laugh. "But you may certainly have the photograph."

"If you marry an engineer you may find that there is a lot of travel in your life," Mrs. Brooks said.

Jennie turned to her in amazement, "Marry an

engineer? What makes you think I'll marry an engineer?"

Mrs. Brooks smiled and said, "Mrs. Hurst tells me you and Jim are corresponding regularly. He is going to ask you to marry him just as soon as he finishes school."

"Well, I don't care if he does ask me." Jennie was angry at the idea that her mother and friend seemed to know more about her business than she did.

"Why don't you send Jim the other photograph?" Mrs. Brooks asked.

"Even if he does ask me to marry him, I don't have to say yes, you know. Jim Hurst is not the only man in the world."

"You're not interested in that reporter, are you?" Mrs. Brooks asked with a worried look. "Reporters don't make very good husbands."

"You needn't worry about that," Jennie answered as she left the room.

That evening she sat under the stars and tried to sort out what her true feelings were. There had been so much change in everyone's life. There was so much loss. First she'd lost her father and then her aunts. Next Jim and Millie were gone. And, yes — she would be honest — she missed Jim a lot. They had grown close just by being together during that dreadful calamity.

And what would life be like when David left? She had grown close to him as well. Jennie told herself that as long as she had her mother and her brother she would be all right.

After a couple of hours of confused thinking, she decided that what she really needed was a good night's rest, and she went to bed.

The next day David was waiting for her at the brickyard with a big smile on his face. "It's come!" he said, and he handed her a telegram to read.

It was a wire from the *New York Times* offering David a position as a correspondent. His first assignment was to be Pittsburgh, where he would cover the trial over liability for the dam breaking.

"That's just the beginning," David said. "I expect they'll send me to London or Paris in the spring. William Randolph says they usually send their most promising young reporters there."

"Congratulations," Jennie said. Now that the news had come, she found she was glad for him.

"Come with me," David said.

"You know I wouldn't consider that," Jennie answered shortly. She would never get used to David's lack of propriety; he just didn't seem to understand what it meant to be a gentleman or what it meant to be a lady.

"As my wife." He took her arms and spun her around to look at him. "I'm serious, Jennie. You can be Mrs. David Winters."

She shook her head quickly, smiling at his childish proposal. David might be a fine reporter, he probably would be famous one day, but he was certainly not anyone she wanted to marry.

"We can be married in Pittsburgh. Right on the courthouse steps." He raised his hands as though to frame in the headline. "Crack reporter weds Johnstown survivor."

"No, thank you." Jennie had to try hard not to laugh. "I certainly don't want to have a front-page wedding."

"But you will marry me?" For the first time, it seemed to occur to David that she might not.

"No, I won't," she said.

"Why not?"

Jennie thought about it for a few minutes before she replied. Even when the words came out of her mouth, she wasn't sure that she meant them or whether she just said them to make it easier for David. "I won't marry you because I'm in love with Jim Hurst."

Chapter
Twenty-five

JENNIE'S job lasted until the middle of August,
and then she was let go on the grounds that there
wasn't much work left. Many of the reporters left
about the same time that David did, and she supposed that the work really was running out. However, she noticed that the one operator who kept
his job was a man.

She never heard from David again after he left,
but Jim wrote her every week. One letter contained
a thank-you for the photograph she had sent him,
and she was puzzled by what he meant. After a few
moments, she realized that her mother must have
given her photograph to Mrs. Hurst to send to Jim.

She would have quarreled with her mother about
meddling, except that she was really quite glad that

Jim had the likeness. In his letter he said that he looked at her photograph every evening before he went to sleep. He also said she was prettier in person than in the photo.

That statement pleased her because she had thought she looked attractive in the photograph. Jim must truly believe she was beautiful.

She got a letter from Millie at the end of July, which said she was now married and that she loved Iowa. As Jennie read on, she noticed that her friend said nothing at all about her new husband or family.

On August twentieth she received another letter from Millie, who sounded very happy, and Jennie breathed a big sigh of relief. Life was hard enough for a woman without an unhappy marriage. Millie wrote a great deal about the lovely countryside and her garden. But she also wrote that her husband was as kind as she had hoped, and that she was finding the children to be a source of joy.

Jennie was reading the letter aloud to her mother when her young brother, Peter, ran in the door and said, "Jim Hurst and his mother are coming."

Mrs. Brooks didn't look a bit surprised as she stood up, smoothed her apron, and pulled the hot apple pie from the oven. Jennie realized that her mother had known that Jim was coming. She was furious. She asked, "Why didn't you tell me?"

Her mother just smiled and went to the kitchen door to greet their guests. Jennie stood behind her, numb with surprise and nervousness as the two older women exchanged pleasantries.

They sat in the kitchen, because there was no

parlor, and talked about things that held little or no interest for Jennie. She could only think about Jim as she tried to look at him without seeming to look at him. Each time her eyes met his, she looked away quickly, blushing as though she'd never seen him before.

Jim looked very grown-up in his new tweed suit, and his eyes seemed to be smiling at Jennie whenever she dared to look his way. He said very little, and Jennie said nothing; they both counted on the older women to keep the conversation going until the pie was gone.

Mrs. Hurst stood up and said, "I must be getting along now. Jim, why don't you stay and talk with Jennie for a while?"

Mrs. Brooks stood up at the same time and said, "Peter and I will walk you home."

So Jennie and Jim were left alone in the kitchen, and Jennie felt as foolish and uncomfortable as if she'd never talked to Jim in her whole life. Finally, when the silence grew too long, she asked, "Are you home for long?"

"A weekend," Jim answered gravely. "I must be back at school on Monday morning."

"Oh." After more silence, she asked, "Would you like some more pie?"

"No. It's enough just to look at you. The photograph really doesn't do you justice."

Jennie laughed and shook her head. "Don't say things like that. It's because of the things that you say in your letters that I'm feeling so shy."

"I mean them all," Jim said quietly.

Jennie looked him square in the eyes and answered, "I believe you do." Then she smiled at him.

Jim seemed to relax as he smiled back, and he asked, "Your friend Mr. Winters has left permanently?"

"Permanently," Jennie assured him. Again, she thought she saw Jim relax, and it occurred to her that he might also be very nervous about this encounter.

"Let's take a walk," Jim said abruptly.

Jennie rose, and the two of them walked down the streets of Johnstown and then upward to the hills. About halfway up the steep climb to the spot where Jim had once kissed her, he took her hand. Jennie did not protest. She felt peaceful and good about being with Jim again.

Once at the top of the hill, they turned to look down on Johnstown as they had once before. She said, "There's been a lot of progress, hasn't there?"

"You were once very angry at me for saying this is the age of progress," Jim responded, "but, Jennie, it is."

He turned toward her, and his eyes were shining as he said, "I know you are a strong person, Jennie Brooks, and I want you to be my wife. Before you answer me, I want to tell you my plans."

She opened her mouth, but he lay his fingers across her lips and smiled down at her. "I have notified the college that I'll be leaving in December. By then, I'll have the technical knowledge I so badly needed to complete my education. And I've written Mr. Matthews, telling him I won't come back to

218

work. Jennie, I'm to have a new life and I want you to share it with me."

Jennie was ready to share any life Jim wanted, but his fingers on her lips prevented her from talking. She could only hope that he could read the truth in her eyes as he told her of his plans. "I have a new position with the United States government. I'm to be an inspector for public safety. New laws will be written, and I'm to enforce them."

Jennie couldn't contain her pleasure. She drew her lips away from his fingers and breathed, "That is wonderful."

His eyes were shining the brightest blue she'd ever seen as he said, "With your help, I'll make this the age of progress for everyone. Just think of it, Jennie. My job will be to inspect dams like the one at South Fork and make sure that they are safely built. Can you think of anything better?"

"Yes," Jennie answered boldly.

Jim was startled, and looked at her in amazement as he asked, "What could be better?"

"It would be better if you kissed me now and talked later," Jennie said, and she lifted her arms to embrace him.

Coming next from Sunfire: DARCY, whose sheltered life as a Galveston, Texas, debutante in 1900 is changed forever by the hurricane that destroys the island — but not her dreams.

SUNFIRE®

Read all about the fascinating young women who lived and loved during America's most turbulent times!